DATE DUE

THE SAVAGE GUN

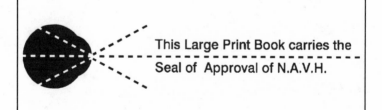

This Large Print Book carries the
Seal of Approval of N.A.V.H.

THE SAVAGE GUN

JORY SHERMAN

THORNDIKE PRESS

An imprint of Thomson Gale, a part of The Thomson Corporation

Detroit • New York • San Francisco • New Haven, Conn. • Waterville, Maine • London

LIBRARY OF CONGRESS CATALOGING-IN-PUBLICATION DATA

Sherman, Jory.
  The savage gun / by Jory Sherman.
    p. cm. — (Thorndike Press large print western)
  ISBN-13: 978-0-7862-9834-1 (lg. print : alk. paper)
  ISBN-10: 0-7862-9834-0 (lg. print : alk. paper)
  1. Large type books. I. Title.
PS3569.H43S28 2007
813'.54—dc22
                                      2007022282

Published in 2007 by arrangement with The Berkley Publishing Group, a member of Penguin Group (USA) Inc.

Printed in the United States of America on permanent paper
10 9 8 7 6 5 4 3 2 1

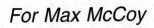

For Max McCoy

1

That morning, John Savage awoke to two kinds of thunder.

There was the thunder already in his head that had lasted through the long night, the pounding thunder that crept into his dreams like ancient tom-toms, blinded him with the throbbing beat of a bass drum, then exploded into a rolling peal of thunder as huge kettle drums, tympani, pounded so loud he screamed until his mother crept to his bed and soothed him to silence.

"My head," he muttered. "The pain won't stop, Ma."

"Now Ben told you not to handle that dynamite with your bare hands, Johnny. He told you to wear gloves."

"Yeah, after I unloaded half a box of that stuff."

"Shhh, you'll wake Pa and your sister. Now, go back to sleep and just bite down on the pain."

"Don't you have some powders or something?" he asked.

"Next time we go to town, Johnny. Now, go to sleep."

He had gone back to sleep, but the drums got louder and the pain shot through his head like an electric current and spread through every nerve in his body until the second thunder awoke him.

This was the thunder of the dynamite explosion in the mine up on the hill above the creek, the one he and Ben had set up to blow the day before.

John scrambled out of his bedroll, groped for his boots in the dim light inside the big tent where he and his family lived along Cripple Creek, high in the Rocky Mountains in Colorado.

He slipped on his boots, laced them up, and crawled from the tent, his eyes two thunderbolts of pain with someone pounding them in their sockets with a ten-pound maul.

The sky was a bloodred smear across the sky as John scrambled up the crude wooden steps fashioned out of whipsawed spruce that led to the mine shaft. Smoke and dust and fine grit weaved through the spruce and fir trees that obscured the adit of the mine, seeping through the coniferous trees like a stain on a wall of green. And he could smell the burnt powder mingled with the scent of evergreens, an acrid odor scratching his nostrils with sharp aromatic fingernails on a witch's long, bony fingers. Clouds wreathed and blanketed the high peaks, their misty underbellies dipping so low, he could almost touch them, and the red sky was like a memory of the explosion itself, smeared like blood across the eastern horizon, a distant ominous painting by a madman flinging gore from a rusted pail.

His parents had not stirred when he left and his sister only moaned in her blankets, still floating in tidal sleep as she always did. And she was always the last to get up and start whining for something to eat. Little Alice, his sister, was nothing but a spoiled brat, ten years younger than he, and, at eight years of age, about as useful in a mining camp as an accordion on a hunting trip.

John's suspenders cut into his shoulders as he cleared the landing at the top and turned to go around the guarding trees, a sudden fear in him that Ben was still inside the mine, his body ripped apart, smashed by hurtling stones into a pulpy mush, every bone broken, flesh mangled, black from fire and unexploded powder.

"Ben, Ben," he called, and rounded the

trees into the choking dust and smoke like a cloud before the adit, like a shroud draping the broken body of his friend whose legs had not carried him from the shaft in time.

"Johnny boy," Ben said, stepping out into the open from a copse of trees that clung to the hillside several yards to the right of the smoldering mine.

"I thought you would wait, Ben. You said you'd wait to blow the powder."

"Ah, couldn't wait. The lure of gold was too great in this hard-rock miner's heart, lad. Besides, it was the best time to light the fuse, see it sizzle and spark as it raced into the darkness. 'Twas a beautiful sight, Johnny boy. I wished you were here."

John, panting, looked at Ben with mingled feelings of anger and annoyance. Anger because Ben had not waited for him before lighting the fuse; annoyance because the man was smiling in triumph, pleased that he had blasted a ton or two of rock with just the flicking touch of match.

"You said you'd wait," John said again, his dark eyes snapping with splinters of light as he batted his eyelids.

"I lied, Johnny. The urge in me was too great, alas. I could not wait. The fuse was set and I did not want dew to settle on it and slow it down."

John, slightly mollified, huffed a huff, snorted a snort, and breathed a deep breath.

"When can we go in?" he asked.

"Soon's all the dust and smoke clears out of that hole," Ben said. He pointed down toward the creek. "Look."

John saw the first tendrils of mist rising from Cripple Creek. As he watched, the mist thickened and rose, spreading to all the miners' tents, forming into clouds like those just above him, fanning out like lush folds of cotton batting, blotting out all the rockers, the sluice boxes, the pans, picks, and shovels that lay along the banks of the creek. The sun was just brimming the horizon, enough to leech all the dew and the moisture from the creek into cloudy vapors that hovered over the camp, shrouding them until all signs of human life and activity disappeared.

"Lovely, ain't it, Johnny?" Ben Russell said.

"Like a dreamworld, almost."

"And the clouds still coming down on top of us. Ain't nature grand?"

"Grand," John said, looking up at the descending clouds, clouds that soon enveloped them in a wispy fog. He could feel the dampness, the soft touch on his face like a fleeting kiss, so soft, it was barely heavier than the air itself.

"The mountains make their own weather. They make the clouds and keep them long as they can, like pups. Then, when the world needs rain, they send them sailing out over the prairies and the dry lands, full of rain. The Injuns hold these mountains sacred and so do I, Johnny."

"So, we're looking at the birthing of clouds right now."

"Yep. And at the nursery. Those cloud-pups will rise up and join the big fellers in the sky. And they'll get fatter and fatter until it comes time to set sail and roam all over the world."

"I like the way you put it, Ben."

"Hell, that's the way it is, Johnny."

Ben turned and walked over to the adit, peered inside.

"You can get one of them barrows over yonder and we can start shoveling."

"Sure," John said. The wheelbarrows were sitting in a copse of spruce and fir trees off to the left of the mine. There, too, were the shovels, picks, adzes, mauls, and some axes in case they had to cut timbers to shore up anything. But so far they had not had to do that. They were into hard rock and hadn't seen so much as a thumbnail of gold. But Ben said there was gold inside there, and

12

they'd hit it any day now.

John loaded a wheelbarrow with two long-handled shovels. He wheeled it toward the mine. There was only room for one wheel-barrow at a time. Ben had blasted perhaps twenty feet into the rock. John didn't know how much deeper he had blown the rock out this morning.

"Safe to go inside, Ben?"

"Yeah, it's thinnin' out. Let me go first, just to check. I'll holler when I'm ready for you to come in."

Ben stepped inside, walked a few paces, then disappeared. The mine was a straight shaft at this point, and would be until they found a vein and had to branch off. John was hoping that today was the day. Ben carried a couple of candles in his overalls and when he got all the way in, he would light one and take a good look at the newly exposed rock wall, going over every inch with a slow patience, like a jeweler examining a precious stone.

John waited, watching the fog build up along the creek, thicken, swell, and rise until he could no longer see any of the tents along either bank. He was glad he was up there with Ben. Gold panning was hard, back-breaking work, and the dry rockers were a chore, as well. And he hated throwing buckets of water into the sluice boxes. It was boring, hard work, too. They had hoses and sometimes siphoned water from the creek into the hoses; that ran pretty well, but this often did not provide enough force to move the gravel through the boxes.

Ben had taught John a secret about finding gold, and he had just put it into practice the night before. He had taken two horse blankets way upstream, away from all the other claims, and tied them together, strung them across the creek, and tied the ends to trees. Ben said that gold would wash down the creek, settle in the blankets, and he could wash them out in a pan and find dust and sometimes nuggets. He planned to check his blankets that evening when they got finished crushing rock and running the gravel through a sluice box. Ben worked for John's father, but he also had his own claim along the creek. They were all working on shares, and so far, his parents and some of the other miners who had come with them had already accumulated quite a bit of dust and several respectable-sized nuggets.

"Oh, Johnny, you can wheel that barrow on in here. I'm going to light one of these candles and just come to the light."

John entered the mine. He could still smell the exploded powder and dust tickled his nose, but it was already settling. He had to bend over, once inside. He saw a flicker of light and headed toward it. His head throbbed even worse inside the mine, perhaps from stooping over. He could barely see through the pain shooting through the backs of his eyeballs.

"Let's take a look," Ben said, holding the candle flame close to the wall. He stood in a pile of broken rock. John had to push the wheel hard to get over some of it. Finally, when he was close enough, he set the barrow down and picked up a shovel. Then he felt woozy, and nearly fell against the wall.

"What's the matter, Johnny?"

"It's my head. It hurts like hell, Ben. Damn you, anyway."

"I told you not to handle them sticks with your bare hands."

"Yeah, after I already had."

"Then, I told you not to touch your hands to your head. I seen you wipe sweat from your forehead. That'll do it ever' time. That stuff Mr. Dupont puts on the sticks gives a man a terrible headache."

"How long does it last?"

"Oh, it'll be gone by this afternoon, I reckon."

"Well, right now, it's like somebody's worked me over with a sledge."

Ben laughed.

As he scoured the wall, John began to shovel ore into the wheelbarrow. The rock made a hollow sound against the wood until the bottom was covered. Then the fragments just made chunking sounds that got duller as the pile got higher.

"Well, looky here, will you?" Ben said, his voice just above a whisper. "I do believe I see yaller gold."

John felt his pulse race. He dropped the shovel and stepped to the wall where Ben held the candle close.

"See it?" Ben said.

John had to strain his eyes, squint them to slits, but he saw it. Small specks of a dull yellow metal embedded in the rock. Then Ben took his shirt sleeve and rubbed a spot nearby. Black soot came off on his sleeve and there, like a splash of yellow paint, was a vein, perhaps six or eight inches long and four or five inches wide.

"Is that gold?" John asked, his headache almost forgotten.

"That be a little lode, Johnny. And where that lode is, could be a streak, and that streak might lead to a great big one."

"I see it. It's beautiful, Ben."

"Run and fetch me an adze, a maul, and a chisel. I'm going to peck around the edges

16

here and see what we got. But we got gold, just like I said we would. Now, don't you breathe a word of this until I show it to your ma and pa. We don't want a bunch of panners running up here and blowing holes in the mountain trying to outflank us."

John was shaking now. He could hardly think. He had seen gold before, but never sticking out of bare rock like this was. His hands started to tremble and his palms slickened with sweat. And he couldn't move his feet.

"Well, what're you waiting for, Johnny? Go and fetch them tools. Take your barrow out and dump the rock where we usually do. You can be crushing rock whilst I look for more vein."

John just stood there, frozen, staring at the gold streak in the wall.

He felt as if he had stepped into another world, a world of riches beyond imagining. The gold hypnotized him, held him in its golden spell, and he never wanted to leave that place and go out into the sunlight where everything he had seen in that dark pit would vanish like the morning dew.

2

There were eight men camped some two miles from Dan Savage's mining claim. They had been there for two days and some of the men were getting impatient. Their leader, Oliver Hobart, had insisted on a dry camp, with no fire to give them away to any who might be watching. They were not even on the creek but below it, and the men there had to sneak up to the creek at night to fill their canteens. They were eating only hard-tack, beef jerky, and canned peaches, and were running low on food, as well.

"Damn it, Ollie, you sure about this Savage feller?" Dick Tanner struck a match on his boot to light his Chesterfield. He was nearing forty, and, like the others, couldn't rub two nickels together. He wasn't as tall as Ollie, who topped six feet in his moldy stockings, nor as muscular, for Ollie was all muscle and hard bone, but he, too, was big and wide in the shoulders, with arms that could crush a hardwood keg into matchsticks. Both men had dark flint eyes and heavy caterpillar brows. People thought they could have been brothers, but they were, in fact, cousins, so the resemblance came natural. They had grown up together and both had learned how to backshoot a man at an early age. Neither one of them was born with a conscience, so killing came easy to them, as easy as stealing or any other crime, for that matter.

"Yeah, Dick," Hobart said. "He's due to pull out for Pueblo tomorrow. Last time he was down, a month ago, he cashed in so much dust he blinded the clerk at the bank."

"We gonna hit this Savage this morning, right?" Mort Anders said. He, like the others, hadn't shaved in a week, and his face was shadowed with beard stubble. He was in his thirties and wanted for murder in at least two states, perhaps three. His pale blue eyes were as cold and dead as a three-day-old mackerel.

"Soon as Pete and Luke get back from glassing Savage's camp and tell me the fog's done lifted," Hobart said.

"Shit, I hate this damned waiting," Fritz Schultz said. He was sitting on a deadfall pine log, digging up the ground with a stick he had whittled to a sharp point. He was wanted for bank robbery and murder back in Kansas.

"Hell, it's free gold, Fritz," Red Dillard said. He was the youngest, at twenty-five, and he had at least five notches on his gun by the time he was eighteen. Red was a small-time thief with an itchy trigger finger. His eyes were blue, also, but blue as the sky and they were never still in their sockets. The man had a nervous tic right below his left eye and he was constantly twitching the other cheek as if to balance things out.

"Not exactly free," Hobart said. "But that bastard Savage and his crew are like beavers on that creek. They're pulling gold out of Cripple Creek faster than old Bob Womack can make it to the assay office in Colorado Springs."

All the men laughed at Hobart's reference to Bob Womack, who had started the gold rush to Cripple Creek in 1890. He hadn't hit it big yet, since he first found some gold up one of the creeks back in '78. But in October 1890, after filing a lot of small claims, he took ore down to Colorado Springs from a new claim. That El Paso lode panned out at $250 the ton, but nobody believed him when he started bragging about it. Men around Denver and El Paso had heard it all before.

But a man named Ed De La Vigne, a mining man, believed Womack, and the following spring, in April of 1891, he formed the Cripple Creek Mining District and Womack got the credit for starting the gold rush.

But Dan Savage had listened to Womack, too, and did some exploring of his own, and Hobart had seen him in El Paso cashing in dust and nuggets. Cripple Creek was choked with prospectors, but few knew about Dan Savage and his claims. Savage wasn't one to brag, as Hobart found out.

"How much dust do you figure Savage has?" asked Army Mandrake, the oldest man in the group. Mandrake was almost fifty and he'd been on the wrong side of the law since he was fifteen, when he murdered his father so he could buy a horse. He'd been on the run ever since, having left Ohio shortly after the murder, and he'd left many a man buried in boot hill because Mandrake didn't believe in working for a living. He had once killed a man for fifty cents. It didn't make any difference to him. He'd sooner kill a man over a bowl of soup than struggle to fulfill his needs. He had coal-black eyes buried deep in his skull and their gaze had chilled many a man at the business end of his Colt.

"It'll be in the thousands," Ollie said.

"More than he had the first time. He's got more men working with him, and he's had more time on that creek."

"How'd they come to name it Cripple Creek, anyways?" Mandrake asked.

"Story is a cow clumped acrost it and broke its leg," Dillard said. "Leastways, that's the way I heard it."

"You heard right," Ollie said. "Bob Womack's family farmed up here nearabouts. That's what got him started looking for gold up all these creeks. I guess he didn't like farmin' much."

The others all laughed, low in their throats, so that they sounded like feral beasts feeding on carrion.

Pete Rutter handed the binoculars to Luke Wilkins, who was lying next to him on large boulder atop an outcropping in the dense forest upstream from Dan Savage's mining camp. Tall pines shielded the pair from being seen by anyone downstream, but there were also spruce and juniper growing nearby, and two large deadfalls in front of them and to the rear that would make it difficult for anyone to reach them in a hurry. Their horses were tied to some pine trees less than a hundred yards away. A thick bank of fog hung over the creek, but the sun was already burning off some of the thin clouds that shawled the mountainside on the other side of the creek.

"Wonder what that explosion was?" Luke asked.

"Miners are always blowing holes in the mountain. Don't mean nothin'," Pete said.

"Sounded damned close."

"It was up on that mountain yonder, but it don't mean they found gold. It means somebody's lookin' for gold."

"I saw the smoke, then them clouds came down, so I couldn't tell rightly where it was."

"Don't worry about it, Luke."

"Yeah, sure."

"Here, take a look, Luke. I still can't see a damned thing. Just a lot of shadows."

"I can hear them moving around down there," Wilkins said, taking the binoculars from Pete.

"Yeah. I think everybody's up by now, but that damn fog's stickin' like cotton candy to the creek and everything on both banks."

"Where'd you ever see cotton candy, Pete?"

"In St. Louis. Carnival come to town when I was a boy and us kids got some for a penny. Man used a bellows to blow the sugar stuff into a big reddish puff. We got it all over our mouths and clothes and Ma like to had a pure-dee fit."

"I had some once't down in N'Orleans. My brother told me it was made by spiders and I wouldn't touch it."

Pete laughed.

"Luke, you're dumber'n a sock full of hickory nuts."

Luke put the binoculars to his eyes, peered at the camp downstream.

"I can see some legs. Oh, there's a shovel. And arms. I can hear that gravel going into the sluice box. And now they've got a bucket brigade goin', a-sloshin' water into that long box, runnin' the sand down over the ribs. Yep, they're working that stream good, Pete. I hope they find a lot of color by the time that fog lifts."

Luke took the binoculars away from his eyes and rubbed them.

"What do you think, Pete? Too soon?"

"To go back and tell Ollie? Yeah. He said don't come until we can see every hair on those boys' skin. Still too much fog."

"But the sun's up now. Should burn off pretty quick, I'm thinkin'."

"Yeah. Should. Been that way nigh ever' day since we got here. Every morning, any-ways."

"You see that sunrise this morning, Pete?"

"Yeah, I saw it."

"Goin' to come a hell of a storm tonight or tomorrow."

"We got slickers."

"Yeah, and rain'll make it hard to track us."

"Well, I think Ollie's going to have something to say about that, less I miss my guess," Pete said.

"What do you mean?"

"You know damned well what I mean, Luke."

Luke's eyes glittered. He was a small, wiry man with close-set porcine eyes and a shock of unruly straw hair. Lean as a whip, he was lightning fast with a six-gun and seemed to enjoy killing human beings. By contrast, Pete Rutter had close-cropped hair with gray streaks at the temples and was a burly, thick-necked man with just the trace of a German accent tingeing his Mississippi drawl. He had murdered a family in Oxford, stole their wagon and poke, sold the wagon in Jackson, and gone to Texas where he continued his life of crime.

They had all met Ollie in Auroria when Hobart was waylaying miners from Cherry Creek and stealing their pokes.

The eight men had seen a bigger opportunity in Cripple Creek when the main street started sprouting gambling halls, saloons, dry goods stores, and the like, and the creek crawled with prospectors. But Hobart had seen a greater opportunity with Dan Savage as a single target. As he told the others, "We can roll drunks until we're all gray-haired, toothless, old coots, or we can get enough gold in one swoop so's we can light a shuck for California and leave these cold, freezing-ass winters behind."

Hobart's plan appealed to all of them, and once they had learned how much gold Savage was taking out of the creek, their greed took hold and they followed Hobart like a pack of pups chasing after a pork chop.

The two men took turns checking the camp with the binoculars. As they waited, the fog slowly began to thin and dissipate. The sun rose high in the sky and they even saw an eagle flying lazy circles far up the mountain, sailing on invisible currents of air like some majestic feathered lord of the skies.

"What do you think, Pete?" Luke asked, after another half hour had passed by.

"Let's give it the better part of an hour. I can see most everybody now, but the tents are still fogged in. I didn't see the little gal or the woman yet. Did you?"

Luke shook his head.

"That little girl sleeps late."

"Yeah, but her mother ought to be hauling a pail down to the creek to dip water out so's they can wash their pretty faces."

"Well, I'll keep lookin'. I don't see that them two are going to make much difference."

"They will to Ollie, Luke."

"Yeah. They will."

Forty-five minutes later, the fog had lifted and they could see the tents, the prospectors lining the bank, some at the water's edge swirling gravel in their pans. Two men were working a dry rocker, which made a lot of noise, and four others were working two sluice boxes, shoveling in gravel and washing it down the chute, then putting the gravel in pans and swishing water until the yellow gold gleamed at the edge of dolomite.

"Let's go, Luke," Pete said. "It's time."

"Yep."

The two slid backward off the rock. Pete slung the binoculars around his neck and led the way back to their horses. The sounds of the mining camp began to subside as they left the rock pile behind. The horses whickered. Luke smacked his horse across the nose to shut it up. The horse bared its teeth and tried to bite him, but Luke thumped him on the lips and the horse backed down, laying its ears flat.

"That horse is going to take a chunk out of you one of these days, Luke."

"If he does, he'll be one sorry horse, I tell you."

Pete mounted up.

Together the two made it back to the outlaw camp where Ollie and the others were waiting.

"Clear?" Ollie asked.

"Clear as a bell," Pete said. "Them boys is working their asses off."

"Let's saddle up, then, and take it slow," Ollie said. "Check your weapons. We don't want no misfires."

They all checked their pistols and rifles. There was the sound of snapping and clicking as they worked the actions, reloaded ejected cartridges, spun cylinders on their six-guns.

"You all wait for my signal when we get there," Ollie said. "Just like we practiced. A solid line of us hits that creek. Then we open up on 'em. You boys on the left take the ones of them on the left and those on the right, take the right. And us in the middle will take out all the runners and crybabies and whiners."

All of the men nodded in assent as they walked to their horses.

After they were all mounted up, Ollie looked them over.

"One thing," he said, "before we go."

They all waited to hear what Hobart had to say.

"Kill 'em all. Ever' damned one of 'em. No witnesses left behind."

"That mean the little girl and her ma?" Luke said.

"Everybody, Luke. You shoot any damned thing that moves. And you all shoot until nothing nor nobody moves."

One of the men swore under his breath, but Ollie couldn't tell who it was.

And he didn't care. He knew the men would do what he wanted them to.

They were as greedy as he was.

3

Dan Savage woke up a few minutes after his son, John, crawled out of the tent. His wife, Clare, stirred, but she was still asleep when he put his boots on and crawled out into the open air. Little Alice was still sound asleep, her rag doll clasped in her arms, her little cherubic face partially covered by her golden ringlets. He touched her forehead and she didn't stir.

Dan turned and looked up into the trees where smoke and dust hung in the air from Ben's blasting. The sky in the east was ablaze with dawn. Long loaves of clouds burned a brilliant red like the sumac and maple leaves in fall. He had never seen such a magnificent sunrise, he thought, and stood there, as if mesmerized, for several moments. The glory of the sky filled him with a reverence he had seldom felt in his life and he wished Clare and Alice were up to see it. He smelled the pines and the acrid smoke as it drifted down from the mine-shaft and exulted in the wonder of it all, as if he had been witness to creation itself.

He stretched and adjusted his galluses, then ran fingers through his hair, pulled on his full beard, then stroked it twice as if to arrange the hairs so that they came to a point. They didn't. He needed a trim, but he would get that done in Pueblo. Clare liked to fuss over him that way, snipping at his hair and beard, but she would be far too busy cooking and packing for the trip on the morrow.

Dan was almost as tall as his son, John, but John had grown an inch or two since they filed their claims several months ago. He was lean and muscular, with a slightly sunken chest, his face and wrists browned by the sun in the clear mountain air. His hazel eyes and aquiline nose gave him a serious look, and with the beard, he might have been taken for a college professor in any eastern town. When he stuck his empty pipe in his mouth, the professorial illusion seemed complete.

Dan walked behind the Marquis tent that was his domicile, over to the bank just above the beach and relieved himself, shooting a yellow stream against the pebbles, small roots of grass, and sand until some of the soil broke loose and joined the small rivulet that flowed down to the sand and soaked in. He and John had built an outhouse in the woods, less than a hundred yards away, but he had no need of it then. They had built it for Clare and Alice, for privacy, but he and the other men used it, too, when they had to perform more complicated functions.

He buttoned his fly and fished a pouch of tobacco from his back pocket. He filled his pipe, spooning tobacco into the bowl with his index finger. A slice of dried apple lay embedded in the loam of the tobacco inside the pouch, imparting a freshness to the rough-cut leaves. He tamped the tobacco with his thumb, slid the pouch back in his pocket, and filched a box of wooden matches from his shirt pocket. He looked for a dry stone, saw one, and struck the match across its rough surface. The match flared and he touched the flame to his pipe, drawing breath through the stem until the small spark ignited. He puffed until the smoke was thick in the air and in his mouth and lungs. Then he walked over to another tent, opened the flap, and peered inside.

The three men inside were just barely awake, their grizzled faces protruding from the heavy woolen blankets that cocooned their bodies. The tent reeked of sweat and tobacco smoke, the fruity scent of dried apricots, apples, and peaches, the lingering aroma of fried bacon and sautéed onions that clung to their stiff soiled clothing.

"Rick, time to turn out of the kip," Dan said to his brother, Richard Savage. "Donny, come on. You, too, Lee."

Donny was Donald French, Clare's brother, and Lee was Leland Russell, Ben's younger brother. They all had shares in the Savage claim, all were in their mid-twenties, not much older than his son, John.

"Is there fog out there?" Donny asked.

"Not as much as there's going to be," Dan said. "We're going to be smothered by a big cloud here pretty quick. Shake it out, boys."

"Damned dynamite woke me up," Rick said. "Lee, your brother ain't got the sense God gave a ball-peen hammer. I swear."

"Ben can smell gold up in that rock," Lee said, tossing his blanket aside like a magician flourishing his cloak.

Dan yelled across the creek to the men in the other tents, friends he had taken into partnership because he knew there was plenty of gold to go around. These were men he trusted, like Gary Whitman, Lou Finley, Jesse Ward, Pat Jensen, and Dale Snider, all single and in their thirties. Good, honest, hardworking men he had hunted with most of his life. Men who thrived on adventure and were at home in the wilderness. All of them were from Arkansas, hillfolk who had originally come from Kentucky with their families, several years after the war.

"Roll out, boys," Dan hollered. "Don't let a little fog bother you."

The tents moved as men's feet flailed against the walls. The fog was moving in, rising from the creek, thickening. But Dan could still see the ground. He picked up a pan and squatted next to the water. He scooped up gravel and sand, began to tip and wobble the pan. Prospecting was like a disease now. He loved the thrill of discovery. He knew the gold was in there, probably deeper than they had been digging and panning.

"This claim will make us rich," he told Clare when he first brought her to Cripple Creek. "Where I'm panning, the creek takes a wide bend and I figure a lot of the gold settled there, over centuries. You'll see."

She had seen. She was even more excited than little Alice when he showed her the first flakes of gold in his pan, like goldenrod dust, shining bright in the sun.

Clare had been raised in the hills of the

Ozarks, so she was right at home in the Rocky Mountains. She was strong and in good health, didn't mind roughing it. She had grown up on a hardscrabble farm, toting water from the branch for her folks, planting taters, and plowing just like her father and brothers. A man couldn't ask for a better wife, a more loyal companion. And they had two fine children to show for twenty years of marriage.

Dan swirled the gravel in the pan, sloshing out the pebbles, adding more water when he needed it. The water was muddy and it took some delicate balancing to swirl out the larger stones and leave only gravel at the bottom. The men across the creek emerged from their tents, went into the woods at various places to pee in private. Dan heard the clatter of a shovel and the groan of a sluice box as Gary and Pat lugged it down to the water's edge.

"Whoeee, look at that sandbar," Gary said, pointing out to the middle of the stream, just this side of the bend. "It done growed during the night."

"You know something," Pat said. "This here crick pans gold even while we catch forty winks."

"You're in a good mood, Pat. Must have had sweet dreams." Gary grinned as he let down the front end of the sluice box.

"I always have sweet dreams. Thinkin' about Julie Belle back home. She'll light up like a Christmas candle when I put a gold bracelet on her wrist."

"Heck, she'll probably marry old Willard Perkins and have two kids by the time you get back."

"No, siree, Julie Belle promised me she'd wait."

Dan listened as all of the men got to work, some on the dry rockers, the others on the sluices. They would work up an appetite by the time Clare called them to breakfast. He swirled the water in the pan. Most of the gravel was gone and now he could see sand. Still no signs of gold yet, although he always imagined he could see it flickering in tiny yellow buds, but he knew that was only his imagination. He sloshed the dirty water from the pan, added a small amount and continued tipping the pan while he moved it in a circular motion. Around and around the water swirled, and out splashed the brownish water until finally he saw the black sand of the dolomite.

He heard the tent flap rustle behind him, turned, and saw Clare and Alice emerge and promptly disappear as they stepped into the fog bank. He heard the crunch of their shoes on the rocks as they made their way to the privy, and in the mountains he heard the screeching of blue jays, the camp robbers, announcing that the cook was up and they could soon fly down and steal crumbs from right under the noses of the humans. The jays were a raucous bunch, Dan thought, but Alice liked to feed them and he liked to hear her laugh when she threw them bits of bacon or biscuit.

Swirl and swirl, the water clearing now, the black dolomite spreading at the lower end of the pan, and then, Dan saw the gold dust begin to cling to the black sand. He moved the pan more gently, letting the gold find its way along the rim of the dolomite and it glowed rich and bright even in the shroud of fog that blotted out the sun.

The fragrance of evergreens wafted down to him as he set the pan down. There was hardly any water left in it. Just the gold and the dolomite. He pulled a small spoon and a small tobacco sack from his pocket. Gingerly and delicately, he spooned the dust from the pan and shook the spoon inside the sack, holding the waxed sides tight against it to scrape away every particle of dust. He parafined the sack so that the dust would not filter through the cotton fibers, a trick he had learned from an old prospector he met in Cripple Creek. Finally, he finished spooning out all the gold dust, sat down and rubbed the small of his back. Panning was hard work, hard on the back, wearing on the eyes. He rubbed them now, but the haze was the fog and the mist that swirled around him, blocking his view of the men working on the other side of the creek, and the boys on his side, who had gone downstream with shovels when last he had seen them.

He heard the clatter of the cooking irons and the clunk of wood as Clare got ready to build a fire. He could hear Alice running back and forth from the tent, bringing skillets and lard and such that her mother asked her for in her sweet, low voice that barely penetrated the cloud that clung to him now, so thick he could barely see his boots.

Up at the mine, he heard the creek of the wheelbarrow and then the clatter of rocks as Johnny dumped it near the big, flat stone he used to smash the ore with one of the mauls. It was a comforting sound. He didn't expect Ben to find any lodes up there, but he had taken Johnny under his wing and Dan thought the older man was a good influence on his son. Ben knew something about hard-rock mining, and they didn't really need either him or Johnny to work the creek. They were sluicing and panning better than a hundred dollars a day by Dan's figuring, some days more, some days slightly less. And they had more than two months of dust in sacks lying in a strong box in Dan's tent.

He heard the scratch of a match and then the whip of flames soaring from the wood. When he turned around he could barely see the fire. His stomach rumbled with hunger and he licked his lips, thinking of the coffee that Clare would soon have boiling. He welcomed that first whiff. The air was chill and just thinking about coffee warmed him some.

And then he smelled it, the coffee, and he heard footsteps on the bridge they had built across the creek. The boys on the other side had smelled it, too, and they were coming over to sit by the fire and be sociable.

Dan stood up.

He turned and walked up to the fire, wisps of fog clinging to him like pearly white cobwebs, then evaporating against the heat of his body.

"It's going to be a beautiful day, Clare," Dan said. "And how's little Alice this morning?" He tousled his daughter's hair.

"I'm not little," she said. "I'm helping Mama."

"You sure are, little darling. Oops, I don't mean little darlin'. Just darlin'."

Clare laughed and the sound was like music to him. He put his arms around her and pecked her on the cheek, just as the other men emerged from the cloud bank and headed for the logs they had laid out to sit on at mealtimes.

Above, at the mine, it was silent, and he wondered when Johnny and Ben would come down. It was very quiet up there. Dan shrugged.

Once they smelled the coffee or the bacon, they'd come down those stairs. No need to call them. They knew where breakfast was.

"How much gold did you find in that pan, Dan?" Gary asked as he sat down on the log.

"Maybe an ounce or more."

"Heck, you can retire then."

All of the men laughed.

Life was good.

And tomorrow they would all head for Pueblo and cash in their dust and nuggets. They would enjoy a short vacation back in civilization.

Clare smiled at him as if she could read his thoughts. And the coffeepot sang, its steam cutting through the mist and becoming part of it. It was just like watching miniature clouds forming right before their eyes on that red-sky morning.

4

A thin scrim of mist still lingered just above the creek, like some ghostly ectoplasm one might see in an old tintype where light had leaked onto the negative through the sides of a camera. Jays chattered in obstreperous squawks as they quarreled over scraps of flapjacks little Alice was throwing joyously into the air like parade confetti on a holiday morning. The aroma of coffee hung in the air, mingling with the scent of fried fatback bacon and aromatic fir trees releasing their fragrance with the evaporating dew.

The eight men in Hobart's gang started blazing away with rifles and shotguns as soon as they emerged from the woods on the other side of the creek. Jays flapped off like blue streaks of light, got sucked into the trees like magnetized filings of cobalt, vanished into bristling green shelters that rose in staggered phalanxes to the blue, cloud-pocked sky. Bright orange flames spewed from angry black and brown muzzles, spitting leaden death at those in Dan Savage's camp who were sitting on logs eating their breakfasts, sipping coffee, laughing, smiling, breathing the cool, fragrant mountain air.

Gary Whitman was just starting to rise from the log when a .44/40 bullet from Army Mandrake's pistol ripped into his left temple at nearly one thousand feet per second. Gary's brains exploded into mush as the projectile passed through his skull, tore half his right ear off, and sprayed Rick Savage with a mist of blood and tissue.

Luke Wilkins found his target in Rick, who started to get up from his perch on the log when he heard the first shot. Rick caught the bullet just below his left armpit. The .50-caliber ball ripped the aorta, mangling his heart. He collapsed in a bloodless heap, dead before he hit the ground.

Hobart shot Dan Savage in the throat just as Dan was opening his mouth to yell out a warning. Blood splashed on Clare's dress like flung ketchup. Hobart shot her in the face and the back of her head flew off like a broken bowl of clabbered milk.

The outlaws splashed across the creek, firing above the splash and spray. The men in Dan's camp began dropping, spinning, sprawling in a macabre dance of death as bullets tore into them like grapeshot, ripping through flesh, gouging through bone.

Little Alice screamed.

That was the last sound the little girl made as a shotgun blast at close range from Pete Rutter's sawed-off double-barreled Browning sprayed her with double-ought buckshot, turning her into a bloody rag doll that fell like a pile of red clothes onto the ground next to the fire. She lay there, her white legs jutting obscenely from her dress, her heart pumping blood from a half dozen holes as her small heart continued to beat.

They called out each other's names, while they were killing. They called each other by name as if they had nothing to fear. They called to each other as if they were shooting milk bottles at a carnival.

"Good shot, Fritz."

"You got him, Ollie."

"Get him, Dick."

The names flew back and forth with each shot.

Dick Tanner and Fritz Schultz downed two men at close range with accurate pistol shots from less than ten yards away. Dale Snider did a half twist, his arms flung straight up over his head, and fell into the cook fire, knocking over the large coffeepot and scattering ashes and coals over the stones around the fire ring.

They all went down: Lou Finley while trying to run away, Jesse Ward as he rushed to pull Mandrake from his horse, and Pat Jensen, who threw his pewter plate at Red Dillard. Ollie Hobart dispatched those who were still twitching with single shots to the head from his Colt .45. The others in the band began to dismount and run toward the tents. They yanked stakes out of the ground and jerked the heavy tarpaulin away, exposing what was inside.

"We found some gold here," Red cried out, after blowing the lock on Dan's strongbox. He held up long burlap sacks, one in each hand, while Mort Anders pulled more sacks out.

"Take down every tent," Ollie shouted, as he put a bullet into Leland Russell's brain just to make sure the man was dead. Donny French tried to crawl to his sister Clare. He was moaning, but still alive. Pete Rutter blasted him at point-blank range with both barrels of his scattergun, turning Donny's chest into ground meat.

"Should we burn everything?" Luke asked.

"No, you damned fool," Ollie said. "You want to bring the town down on us? Just get the gold and let's get the hell out of here."

The outlaw gang ransacked every tent, looking for gold. They turned out the pockets of the dead men, and Pete found the sack of dust Dan had panned that morning and stuck it in his shirt pocket.

"That all of 'em?" Ollie asked, looking around at the dead sprawled there like broken mannequins.

"We got ever' last one," Mort said.

"Then, let's light a shuck," Hobart ordered.

The outlaws splashed across the creek, vandalizing the tents on that side. It only took a few moments. They found no more gold, and disappeared into the pines, leaving a scene of carnage on the opposite bank as the sun blazed down on blood and body parts. Flies swarmed over the bodies and, high up in a pine tree, a jay screamed and took to the air, a flitting blue light against the green of the trees.

Ben heard the gunshots and at first he thought they came from some kind of celebration with Chinese firecrackers popping off. He was chiseling around the streak of gold on the wall, while John was breaking open a chunk of rock on the floor of the cave that was flecked with gold and showed promise.

"What's that?" John asked, looking up at Ben.

"Damned if I know. Wait here."

Ben threw down his hammer and chisel and rushed to the mine entrance. He stepped outside and stood peering through the trees at the slaughter below.

John came rushing up, then, and stood by Ben.

"My God, Ben. We've got to get down there."

John started to run around the trees when Ben grabbed him by the back of his shirt and pulled him back into the trees.

"You go down there, you'll wind up dead as them, Johnny."

"But they're killing everybody."

"I know," Ben said softly. "And we don't have so much as a slingshot between us. Just wait. Look at their faces. Study them."

"I can't just stand here."

John saw his mother go down, then saw his sister hurled to the ground by a blast from a shotgun. Tears rushed from his eyes, flowed down his cheeks in hot freshets. He began to shake with fear and rage.

The voices of killers floated up to them like disembodied fragments of sound on a

47

gramophone record.

"Get him, Lukey. Shoot his ass."

"I got him. Boy, I got him good."

"Hey, Pete, you done good on that one."

"Look at the men doing this," Ben said softly. "Don't look at — at them you love and know, Johnny."

John saw his father, saw the big man ride over and shoot him again. He forced himself to look at the killer's face.

"Listen to their names, Johnny. Remember their names. Put the names to their faces." In a soft voice, Ben said these things as Johnny stared at the murderers. He felt as if he were in a kind of trance, that none of what he was seeing was real but the loud explosions of the guns, the white smoke, the sparks like a thousand fireflies in the harsh glare of daylight, the falling bodies, the blood; all these things brought reality hammering into him like a boxer's fists, and each death tore at his heart, wrenched it from its moorings until it hurt so deep the pain was part of him as tears streaked his cheeks, falling unchecked from wide-open eyes.

"Hey, Red, how'd you like that shot?"

"Mort, you got a dead eye, whooeee."

He heard their names and put their names to their faces as they slaughtered his friends and his family and he screamed out silently for justice, for some force to come down from above and kill all the killers, slay all the slayers, blow them to pieces, smash them to bits for what they were doing, for the enjoyment they showed on their pasty brutal faces. The men appeared vivid to him, with dirt rings on their necks, sweat stains at their armpits, their wrinkled, slept-in shirts and trousers, their worn galluses, their scuffed and grimy boots, the clinking rowels on their spurs, the flash of gunmetal on their pistols and rifles.

He observed them as they tore down the tents and winced when the lock was blown off his father's strongbox, felt his stomach collapse when he saw them snatch the bags of gold up and display them like beheaded trophies, or dead ducks blown from the sky in a cloud of lead.

He saw them stalk the shore, ripping, pulling, jerking, snatching all the tent stakes and throwing the canvas down like dirty laundry, saw them kick and knock over every standing thing as if bent on destruction for destruction's sake. And their guns went silent, slipped back into holsters and scabbards, and still he stared at every face, memorized every movement of their hands, studied their faces for any sign that they might have human souls somewhere inside their sweating, oily bodies.

John stopped trembling when the men splashed across the creek and disappeared into the trees. But the sound of gunfire still echoed in his mind and he could smell the burnt powder as if it had been rubbed under his nose. He could still see, somewhere in the darkest shelves of his mind, the falling men, the friends stopped from running, from calling out, from screaming in pain, from breathing. And he could smell the blood, too, smell it like spilled wine on a table coated with candlewax and crushed peaches, the pulp of mashed pears and the decayed meat of persimmons.

The silence filled up all the space around Ben and John as they stood there behind the trees, dumb witnesses to horrible, almost unmentionable crimes of humanity since time immemorial. The silence was like a leaden weight on the morning, a hidden element of sunshine, the silvery glisten of the softly sobbing creek, the overpowering scent of blood and pine sap.

He stared at the scattered debris where the tents had stood, the woolen blankets, the leather saddles and saddlebags, the stringy remains of bridles, the ropes, and all along the shores, the broken sluice boxes and rockers, the shovels lying like broken sticks, the picks, hatchets all strewn as if an army had passed by and cast off its weapons and accoutrements on a deserted battlefield. It was all so desolate and austere, like a landscape left behind a passing plague that took all life with a single breath of wind.

"Ben, my God, look at that down there," John said, a dazed look in his eyes, a numbness of disbelief in his toneless voice. "They — they're all dead. All of them. Dead."

Russell sniffed the air as if to test John's words on the breeze that sighed through the pines and the spruce and the fir. The sun was midway to its zenith, the air warming even the cool shade of the place where they stood, holding back the dankness of the mine at their backs. He shook his head, blinked his eyes, fisted them shut tight, then opened them again to stare in bewilderment at the broken bodies strewn over the garbage that had once been their living quarters, their homes, their peaceful night beds.

"We've got to go down there, Johnny. We're going to have to look at them and lay them to rest, God bless their eternal souls and damn those who took their breaths."

"I-I can't," John said.

"Then I'll go. You stay here."

John recovered some of his senses and

said, "No, Ben, I mean I can't believe they're all dead. Maybe . . ."

"We must go and see, Johnny."

"Yes."

They walked out of the trees like men stumbling from the epicenter of a terrible storm, Ben in the lead, John following close behind. They climbed down the steps in slow motion, filled with a dread in their hearts that weighed them down, turned their feet into useless slabs of heavy stone.

On firm ground, both men turned and stood there, gazes fixed on the dead bodies they must approach, and unable to take the few more steps it would take to cover the space dividing them. Ben's eyes filled with tears and he wiped his sleeve across his face, trying not to choke on those tears he held back, tears that caught in his throat like swallowed fish bones.

He took John's arm and together they walked over to the still smoldering fire that stood at the center of the abattoir. John looked down at his little sister and doubled up with grief, his sobs ripping from his throat in a terrible scream of mourning. And then he saw his mother, her sightless eyes frosted over, glinting with sunlight, vacant, dead, as fixed as dried resin set in polished glass.

"Mother," John breathed, and fell upon her lifeless body, clasping her shoulders, pulling her to him as if he could give his life for hers, as if he could make her whole again.

As he lay there, John could not stop crying.

And that was the only sound in the awful stillness of the waning morning.

5

Ben knelt down next to the body of his brother, Leland. He lifted his brother's limp hand, saw the dirt embedded under the fingernails, felt the knobs of his calloused knuckles, the cords threading his palm.

"Oh, Lee," Ben said. "Oh, dear, sweet Lee, I'm sorry."

He could barely look at the others, but he forced himself to scan their bodies in the distant hope that one might still be alive. The bodies lay still, flies buzzing at their nostrils and eyes, penetrating their ears, crawling over their mouths and faces. A jay landed on an overturned skillet, its eyes shining like polished beads, its head twisting around in jerky movements. Another jay flew down, landed a few feet away, and strutted across the gravel, its head tilted as it eyed the ground for crumbs.

Ben stood up and shaded his eyes as he peered upward at the sun. Its rays felt warm

on his skin and there was something benefi-
cent about its golden glow on his face, as if
life could be renewed in some magical way
just by letting the sunshine seep over his
skin and penetrate the flesh, restoring vital-
ity to flaccid muscles and limp tendons. He
was alive. His brother Leland, and all of his
other friends, Sam and Clare and little Alice, all were dead and no elixir, no potion,
no radiance of sun, could bring any of them
back to life. They were dead and gone, when
a few moments before they had all been
smiling and talking, breathing the crisp
mountain air.

Ben swore under his breath and watched
as John arose from his mother's breast and
stumbled over to Alice. John stooped down
and picked up the blood-spattered body of
Alice, held her in his arms as he would hold
a broken doll. Alice's golden blond ringlets
hung from her head like ribbon remnants
from a long-ago birthday party, and they
held their sheen in the sun. Blessedly, her
eyes were closed and she looked at peace,
as if she was merely asleep and John was
carrying her to her bed.

"I'm real sorry, Johnny," Ben said, shifting
his weight from one foot to the other, his
hands dangling helplessly at his side.

"Poor little Alice," John said. "She was so

pretty, had so much to live for. She loved life so much." He choked on the last few words and could speak no more as fresh tears flooded his eyes and coursed down his face, twisting and overrunning the tracks that were already there.

"We could get the wagon and take everybody to Colorado Springs, Johnny. They got an undertaker there. Or, if you like, we can haul 'em to Pueblo. A lot farther. Maybe easier. I don't know."

John lay Alice's body out on the white tent canvas he had just smoothed out with his boots. He picked up a blanket and covered her with it. Jays marched around like little blue martinets just on the edge of where the camp had been.

"No, we'll bury everyone up in that meadow, beyond where we built the barn and keep the wagons. You know the one I mean?"

"Well, yeah, that's a mite purty place, Johnny. Ground might be soft there. It's got a spring."

"It's got a spring, a little creek, some columbines growing. Pa always talked about building a house up yonder. He and Ma both. He took a claim on it in my name. It's got a good view of the mountain ranges on both sides, lots of green grass and flowers.

Alice would love to be buried there."

"Your ma, too, Johnny. You're right. That'd make a nice, fine place."

"And, someday, maybe I'll build a big old house there and we'll already have a little cemetery. There's some junipers and some spruce down on the lower far corner that would make a fine little cemetery."

Ben could see that John was holding it all in, talking faster than a Cherry Creek magpie just so he wouldn't have to think about what he had seen with his own eyes, what he was never going to forget for as long as he lived.

"Why, I think that's a right nice place, Johnny. I know my brother, Lee, would be proud to buried there alongside your kin and all his friends. I'll walk up to the barn and hitch a couple of mules to the wagon and come on down here. We can get them all in maybe two loads. I think we can shorten the digging time a heap, too, if you agree to my idea."

"What's that, Ben?"

"We'll get us a few sticks of Dupont sixty/forty, cut 'em in half, cap 'em, lay 'em out the way we want the graves to be, set 'em all off. The nitro will blast each plot and we can dig out what needs be dug out."

"Good idea," John said. "Bring the wagon

down. I'll lay everybody out and cover them decent."

"You be all right, John?"

"Yeah. Go on. You know, Ben, those bastards didn't get all the gold we had. And they didn't get something else, something just about as precious to me."

"What's that?" Ben stopped on his walk up to the path that would take him to the meadow through a fringe of trees along a ridge.

"My daddy's gun."

"You mean that fancy Colt of his? I thought he kept that in a lockbox at the bank in Pueblo."

"Nope. He gave it to me, and I buried it in a little strongbox, along with my poke."

"You got a poke?"

"I been keepin' that, too. For a long time. Remember that muley I killed last year up at timberline?"

"Yeah. I remember you skinnin' it and tannin' it out. Liked to drove your mama plumb crazy, all that lye, that burnt wood soaking, the smell of the hide when you boiled it."

"I made leather pouches out of that hide and I've been filling them with dust and nuggets Alice and I panned from the creek when the rest of you was drinking peach brandy and hollering while you danced on the wagon sheets after sundown."

"Well, that's right smart of you, Johnny. I got a poke, too, smarty-pants. Been keepin' it in a box I buried up by my mine. Looks like you and I aren't paupers, exactly, are we?"

John grinned.

Ben tossed John a wave and started hiking up the wagon-rutted road. John turned to the task at hand, going to his mother next, picking her up and carrying her over to the flattened tent, laying her beside Alice, covering her up with the same wide blanket.

He looked at his father and winced when he saw the wounds. He fought back the tears, but his ducts filled up anyway. Some fell on his father's face as he lifted his lifeless body from the ground and carried him over to the canvas. He laid him out next to his mother and retrieved another blanket from the detritus and covered his face and body, leaving only the boots sticking out.

While he was attending to his grisly task, John kept seeing the faces of killers. He put names to their faces, ran names and faces through his mind over and over until they were indelible. He looked down into the creek when he crossed the bridge, looked into its swirling amber-green water flecked with gold and silver from the sun and he listened to its soothing babble as if it were some kind of cryptic symphony that filled the empty spaces in his heart. The screeching of the jays, too, seemed to be speaking to him in strange, mournful tongues, and even the solemn trees rising to the sky seemed fraught with hidden messages of life and death, of ordinary matters and of those things arcane and indecipherable in the course of human history. He felt strangely light-headed and heartsore, as if all of his vital organs had been cut out of him and lay strewn along the creek bank with all of the other things pertaining to mundane, everyday life, a diurnal account seemingly suspended in time, outside of his mind's grasp, elusive, like the tiny rainbows that danced in the stream as it bounded over smooth and shiny rocks, shooting spray into the air that quickly vanished in the small corner of the universe that lay scattered around him like remnants of some somber dream.

By the time John heard the wagon top the ridge and start down the road, its wheels rattling, its wood groaning, he had laid out all of the bodies and covered them. He'd had to cross the bridge to gather up more blankets from the other side of the creek, but all of the corpses were covered, and John felt enervated from the effort and the mental strain. He had never seen a dead person before, and to have seen so many, all at once, was very nearly overwhelming.

Ben pulled up in the wagon, turning it around so that it faced back toward the ridge. He set the brake and climbed down. He looked at all the blankets, so still, so final. A light breeze lifted the corner of one blanket and it flapped like a loose shutter. Jays quarreled with shrill screeches over by the campfire that John and Ben put out by pouring water and sand over it. Chunks of kindling and cut logs lay scattered nearby as if some great beast had run through the camp and knocked them askew.

"Tough job, Johnny," Ben said. "But you done it. You ready to go up? I'll throw in some shovels and we can start loading."

"Yeah, I guess. I think we ought to get our guns first. Just in case. Don't you?"

"I reckon they didn't take anything with 'em but the gold. Seen my rifle anywhere?"

John shook his head.

"I didn't look," he said and now started scanning the barren ground where their tents had once stood. There was so much debris, no single item stood out. There were kegs and wooden canteens, lanterns, hatchets, various other tools, tins and airtights, clothing, utensils, pots, pans, a torn flour sack, another of beans, an open coffee tin, nails, hammers.

Together, Ben and John poked through the scattered goods, finding scissors, needles and threads, yarn, bolts of cloth, odd pieces of leather, an awl, Alice's wooden toys, a couple of small dolls she liked, all kinds of things that tore at John's heartstrings and made him sick to his stomach.

Wrapped in an old army blanket that was moth-eaten and faded to a whitish gray, John found his father's Winchester '73, a .30-caliber lever action that shone like a crow's wing in the yellow sunlight. There were two boxes of cartridges inside, as well. The blanket had been beneath an over-turned cot. The scabbard, John knew, was up at the log barn they had built the summer before, locked up in the tack room with the saddles, bridles, hackamores, and halters they had carried all the way from Arkansas so long ago.

"I found my rifle, Johnny," Ben said, holding up his heavy Henry Yellow Boy, its bluing all mottled and the brass shining like pure gold. "They didn't see it, likely, under a pile of empty flour sacks I been meaning to make me some shirts from bye and bye."

"We can gather all the guns later," John said. "I'm sure they're all here under all this stuff."

"You get your pistol? Your poke?"

"No, not yet."

"Maybe you should."

"I don't have a holster for it yet."

"Lee had him a holster. Made it hisself over the winter. He was going to buy him a Colt the next trip down the mountain over to Pueblo."

"I wouldn't know where it is," John said, his voice sounding dull and faraway to himself.

"Get the pistol and we can look for the holster later."

John drew in a deep breath, held it for a long moment. There was no need for secrecy anymore. He would not have to hide his poke nor his pistol from anyone. There wasn't anyone to hide these things from. It was still hard to imagine they were all gone. But they were. He looked over at the blankets and his eyes fisted shut as the tears started to well up again. Would he ever stop crying? Not this day. There was still the burying to do. And that would be hard. Hard as anything he'd ever had to do. Little Alice. His ma. His pa. All of his friends, and Ben's brother, his mother's brother.

"I got the rifle," John said, opening his eyes. "I'll get the pistol later. Ain't nobody goin' to find it." He said the last sentence almost belligerently, as if challenging Ben. But Ben had no interest in his poke or his pistol. He knew that. It was just that he had to give up the only secret he had and he wasn't quite ready to do that yet. He would dig up the box later. He knew right where it was.

He heard the clank of shovels striking the bed of the wagon. He saw Ben put his Yellow Boy under the seat, heard the swish of the mules' tails as they swatted flies, saw their ears twitch, heard one paw the ground with its hoof. The creek swished against its banks in a whispery undertone and he heard the flap of a jay's wings as it braked for a landing nearby.

"We got eleven to carry, Johnny. Want to take your folks, my brother, and your uncle with the first load, then come back for the others?"

In a fog of unbearable grief, John answered.

"Yeah, Ben, that would be fine. Let's just do it."

Ben's eyes squinted at John's unnatural tone of voice. He looked at John, his eyes hard as agates, an unspoken question flitting in their depths.

John felt something hardening in him, something that had not been there before. He didn't know what it was, but he had an indication when he began to see the faces of the outlaws again when he looked up at the green trees and the blue sky and the white puffs of clouds floating in a serene sea high above the earth. He saw their faces and felt that same something tighten in him. It wasn't hatred, exactly, it was something beyond that simple explosive emotion.

It was more like resolve, or determination, or something that had no name as yet.

He didn't know what to call that hard thing growing in him, but he knew what it was steeling him up for, all right.

He was going to hunt down Ollie and the others, one by one, if necessary. He was going to hunt them down and kill them the same way they had killed his family and all of the good men now lying dead under those breeze-ruffled blankets.

And each one, he vowed, was going to know why his life was being taken.

He walked to the front of the wagon and lay the Winchester and the cartridge boxes next to the Henry.

He knew then what that hardness was that was forming and growing inside of him.

It was the gun, the six-gun, the beautiful Colt his father had given him. It was the gun.

The gun that he would ever live by, henceforth.

6

A pair of blue-winged teals flew up the creek on whistling wings. A chipmunk ventured down to the campsite seeking crumbs, its caramel stripes rippling on its furry coat as it stopped, sat up, then crept forward again, its bright eyes glittering, tail flicking with nervous twitches. A small cloud passed over the sun as John and Ben lifted the body of Clare Savage onto the wagon bed. John had folded her arms across her chest after he removed the blanket.

He pushed a lock of her hair away from her face, and something lodged in his throat, shut his breath off for a moment. He closed his eyes and sighed.

Next, they loaded little Alice, placing her next to the body of her mother. Her arms were folded the same way. John did this with each body, his father Dan's, his uncle Donny's, Ben's brother, Lee. The cloud slid away and sunlight sprayed John's taut features with sudden light that illuminated the grim cast to his expression, as he and Ben covered the bodies with blankets. Ben pulled down the brim of his hat to shade his eyes from the sudden glare.

Ben's facial expression was no less grim than John's as he gently closed the tailgate. A jay berated the chipmunk with a stream of avian invective. The chipmunk barked a series of raspy bleats as it picked up a small piece of biscuit, sat up straight, holding the crumb in its tiny hands. It began to nibble on the crumb, tail flicking back and forth like a bristling metronome.

"Take your seat, Johnny," Ben said.

John didn't answer. He walked to the front of the wagon and climbed up, sat on the spring seat. It groaned under his weight. He looked up at the trees, the play of light on the pine needles that protruded like viridian tassels, their shades of green changing from light to dark as the other limbs swayed in the breeze. He looked at the eternal mountains that rose snow-peaked in the distance, as if searching for something permanent, some monument to life that could overcome death. The solemn trees stood like silent mourners above the creek, their branches swaying gently, back and forth, as if they were waving farewell to the muted beat of music no human could hear.

The wagon trundled up the road, jouncing over the ruts. John had helped Ben in the building of it. They had dug trenches along each side to mark the width of the road itself. Ben had cut dynamite sticks in half, placed them four inches apart while John watched the way he did it. Ben placed caps in each stick, burying them in the sawdust laced with nitroglycerin. Then he had cut fuses to length. When Ben lit the fuses, they both had run and hid behind large boulders. When the dynamite blew, rocks and earth hurtled through the air with deadly force, smashing trees, crashing into the rocks where they were concealed. When it was over, they had two drain trenches along either side. And a road. John had been fascinated with dynamite, but had never handled it until Ben thought he was ready. But he had failed to wear gloves and now he had a king-sized headache. His head was throbbing still.

"There's a pair of gloves on the floorboards, Johnny, and a knife you can put on your belt."

"I'm going to cut the dynamite?"

"If you want to."

"I do." John picked up the gloves and slipped them on. They were made of leather, tawny deerhide, and they fit him. He took the gloves off, shoved them in his back pocket, and picked up the knife.

"Found it in the tack room when I was looking for some rope to use when we do the buryin'. Your daddy must have left it there when he was last up to the barn."

"I recognize it."

It was a beautiful skinning knife his father had made back in Arkansas. It had a deer-antler handle that fit his grip perfectly. He had made the blade from an old wagon spring, and drilled through a chunk of brass for the guard that curved up on one side, down on the other, just like an old pirate's cutlass, or so John imagined. He had always admired the knife and begged his father to make him one just like it. But Dan had never found the time. The scabbard was homemade, too, sewn with sinew, sturdy leather taken from one of their Poland China hogs.

"I don't have my belt on," John said, realizing how incongruous it sounded. But just then, everything was incongruous. Everything he saw and felt seemed out of place, of no consequence, slightly off-kilter. He tried to shut out thoughts of the dead lying in the wagon like so many waxen figures under blankets.

A bald eagle rose in the air from its perch above the creek, the wind catching its pinions and flinging it into an air current that would sail it over the land like an errant kite, the fan of its tail feathers shifting, adjusting to every whispering whiff of breeze, the tips of its wing-feathered fingers grasping for purchase on a ledge of wind.

The wagon rumbled onto the green meadow that lay at the end of a long valley. On the high end rose a majestic mountain peak, its top clad in ermine-white snow. Tall pines bordered the meadow on both sides and at the top. At the bottom, there was a sloping drop-off that led to the creek below. Hobbled horses, more than a dozen, grazed in various places on the greensward. Some lifted their heads and whinnied at the mules, others switched their tails and shook their heads up and down, tossing their long manes into the wind that blew them into wild fragments that settled back down on their necks. A red-tailed hawk floated above the trees, its head moving robotically from side to side as it hunted field mice or conies, and its shrill cry pierced the silence like a referee's whistle, the sound torn to shreds by the high wind that floated him on cushions of air.

Ben headed the wagon toward the barn

and corral on the near side of the meadow.

"Pick up the dynamite, caps, and fuses," he said laconically. "Got 'em set out."

John nodded, caught up in the beauty and grandeur of the land, the sky, the towering mountains silhouetted against a blue, cloud-flecked horizon high above timberline.

He slipped his gloves on and helped Ben load the half-full box of dynamite. Ben placed a box of caps and a fuse coil under the seat next to their rifles, then climbed back up on his perch. John hauled himself up, and after he sat down, the wagon rolled toward the other side of the vale, just off the foot of the bottom end.

The two men were silent as they crossed the small creek, splashing through its amber-gold waters, and pulled up next to a copse of spruce and fir trees. Beyond, John knew, there was an open place of shade and serenity, an untouched garden amid the tall pines.

Ben reined the mules to a halt, after twisting the wagon into a half turn, and set the brake.

"This the place you had in mind, Johnny?"

John nodded.

"Figured. Nice place."

"Let's do it," John said, that hard, cold place in him darkening, getting colder, harder as those terrible images of men shooting down his family and friends in ice-laced blood. The precision of it. No missed shots. No ricochets. No wild bullets flying in space. Every shot hitting home, drawing blood, smashing bone and flesh, crushing beating hearts, tearing up lungs and wind-pipes, blowing black holes in faces and bod-ies. The horror of it emblazed on his mind like painted figures on the cave walls of his mind, as vivid as if it had all happened seconds ago, as if it were still happening.

"I'll lay it all out," Ben said. "You cut me a dozen sticks. Don't touch your forehead with them gloves."

John took the box of dynamite from the wagon. He drew the knife from its sheath, knelt down and began to gently saw through each stick, cutting each one exactly in half until he had twenty-four half sticks laid out in a neat row. A small gray bird flitted in the brush just outside the glade, chirping as it landed on each new branch. John saw it out of the corner of his eye, and then it was gone, like some ghost bird, leaving only a gnawing silence as if some silent thing was eating at the far fringes of his mind.

"Bring 'em over, Johnny."

John scooped up the sticks, carried them in his arms over to where Ben had shoveled twenty-four depressions in the earth. There was the smell of moss and pinesap, the aromatic fragrance of spruce and fir, the delicate scent of a lone blue columbine just catching the sun at the edge of the meadow like some small and forlorn orchid sprouted for just that moment.

"I'll cap 'em and bury 'em. You bring me that coil of fuse in the wagon."

"The explosion's going to ruin this place, Ben."

"No. Not the way I'll do it. We'll still have some digging to do. Not much, I hope."

John went back to the wagon and got the length of fuse, carried it to where Ben was kneeling in the shade of the trees. Ben buried each stick deep so that only the very top was visible. He carefully pushed a cap into the center of the sawdust mixture. John watched him. He knew that the caps were dangerous. If one went off while Ben was pushing it down into the dynamite it would blow his hand and arm off, a grisly thing to contemplate just then.

When Ben was finished, he measured the fuse, counting off seconds in his mind. Shadows shifted in the glade, appearing and disappearing, stroking the grass like shadowy fingers, pulling away, then pushing back over soft green grass and dank moss, the coarse bark of the trees.

Ben walked the end of the fuse away from the planted sticks of dynamite, to the edge of the meadow. He stopped and looked around for a place to hide.

"Better drive the team up the meadow and as close to the trees as you can get. Just wait there. Crouch down in front of the seat and put your fingers in your ears. Take that box of dynamite with you."

"What about you?"

"I'm going to run into the woods. See that big old rock over there? I'll hunker down behind it. You'll be all right where you are. Most of this stuff's just going to plow ground underneath it. Be a few small rocks, maybe, flying like bullets. But they won't go far. A hundred yards or so, I figure."

"You're the powder man," John said.

"That's what I am, Johnny. Now git."

John walked over to the wagon, carrying the unused coil of fuse with him. He set the box of dynamite and the fuse material into the wagon and climbed up, released the brake. He drove the wagon far up the meadow, nearly five hundred yards from where Ben stood, waiting to light his match. After he stopped, he looked back, then doubled over in the well beneath the seat. He waited, the stillness around him as deep as a mountain well back home.

The explosion was nothing like the one he'd heard that morning when Ben blew the wall inside the mine. This one made a deep *whump* sound, and then he heard the rain of dirt and rock through the trees like hail hitting a sod roof. He raised up and saw white smoke hugging the grass, creeping though the trees, billowing out into the air. The wind caught the smoke and severed it into wispy scarves that pirouetted in graceful arabesques until they vanished against the blue of the sky.

He drove back down the meadow to where Ben stood waiting for him. They took their shovels and began to scoop the loose earth out of the wide depression created by the blast. They dug into soft earth until they struck rock and could delve no deeper.

"Not six feet," Ben said, "but they ought to be all right here. Bears and wolves won't be able to smell 'em, and we can haul rocks in here to put over the graves. That all right with you, Johnny?"

"I reckon. I don't want to think about it right now."

Ben softened.

"I know."

They carried the bodies, which had become stiff by then, into the glade. They wrapped the corpses in blankets until they resembled large cocoons and laid them side by side, packing them close. They had five more bodies to haul up there. But there was room for those they had left behind.

"I can cover them, Johnny, if you want to sit down somewheres by yourself."

"No. I'll help. They're gone. I can't bring 'em back."

Ben looked at the young man who had been growing old before his eyes. He felt the hardness in the youth, and he thought he could see that dark place where his soul had gone. He said nothing, but he knew that could be a dangerous sign in one so young as John Savage. Life shaped a man, and some men bent under its withering winds, its freezing chills. But a strong man weathered the bad times and grew taller and straighter and stronger. He hoped Johnny Savage was such a man. But he knew that this was a turning point in his life, a dangerous crossroads in light of all that had happened that day.

He watched as John got the shovels and brought them back, handing one to him. He stood there for a moment, his shovel at the ready, watching John start to throw dirt onto one of the bodies. Beneath the flung dirt lay Dan Savage. John had started the burying with him, his father.

Ben started shoveling loose dirt onto the corpses at the other end, his own brother and Clare's brother. For a long time there was only the sound of dirt spattering onto the blankets, and the wind sobbing through the trees, the far-off piping of a quail and the eerie whistle of a young bull elk.

It was late afternoon when the two men finished burying all the dead. Neither had eaten all day, but neither did they hunger for food as they finished tamping down the mounds of dirt that formed a single grave for eleven people.

"Do you want to say a prayer, Johnny?" Ben asked.

"No."

"Do you want me to say one?"

"It don't make no difference to me. They can't hear you."

There was that hardness in John, Ben thought. Getting harder all the time.

"I thought the prayer was for God," he said.

"I already prayed in my mind, Ben. I don't need to hear no words."

John had become almost primitive in his speech, Ben thought. Laconic. Like his namesake, a savage.

"All right, Johnny. I'll just say this, and be

done with it."

Ben cleared his throat and took off his hat. He bowed his head and closed his eyes.

"Lord, take these good people into your Heaven. They done nobody no harm. Take care of 'em. Amen."

"Good enough," John said.

Large, white billowing clouds rose from behind the snowcapped peaks, wafting slowly toward the prairie. They cast shadows across the meadow, towering high in the heavens, all fluffy and serene, looking soft as eiderdown, peaceful as a quiet summer afternoon. The two men put their shovels into the wagon and climbed in. They drove to the barn and unhitched the mules, grained them, and turned them onto the pasture with hobbles on their front legs.

Neither man spoke as they walked down the road toward the deserted and desolate camp. Their rifles rested flat on their shoulders, balanced there as if on fulcrums. John carried a box of .30-caliber cartridges in his left hand, his knife and scabbard in his right.

The sun disappeared behind the high snow of the thunderheads and a pair of doves whiffled past on whirring wings, twisting and turning in the air like feathered darts. They were mourning doves, the most gentle of birds, he thought. Ben looked at them as they winged past. John did not.

Ben sighed. Worry lines furrowed his forehead.

As the twig is bent, he thought, so grows the tree.

John's shoulders drooped. Ben thought he looked like an old man at that moment.

He hoped that John would also turn out to be a wise man, young or old.

7

Thunderheads lined the sky: great, towering white behemoths stretching from north to south, east to west, blotting out the sun, casting a giant shadow over the land. The creek waters turned from amber and gold and silver to a sullen murkiness of dark umber and coal black, running fleet with somber waters.

"I'll rig us up one of these tents," Ben said. "Clear up some of this mess. You want to build us a fire? We need to cook some grub."

"Sure," John said, laying his rifle down on a rock higher up the slope above the campsite. He walked to the fire ring and held his hand over it to see if there were any coals left. There was no heat, only charred wood and ashes. He began to pick up the scattered sticks of kindling that lay strewn from the place where they had been stacked.

Ben walked some yards away to a tent that

had not been spattered with blood. He gathered up the poles, pulled the top of the tent up and propped it with first one pole, then the other. He pulled the tent tight, and then searched for a hammer to drive in the stakes to give the tent its shape and stability.

A small flock of green-winged teals streaked low over the creek, heading south along its winding course. They flared out of formation when they saw the two men, then quickly rejoined their mates, their wings keening like silver whistles as they knifed through the air and became like mere whispers heard in passing.

John built a pyramid of sticks, started shaving one with his knife, flicking the dry chips into the base of the cone. When he was finished, he walked over to Ben.

"Borrow your matches?" he said.

Ben fished a box from his pocket, handed them to John, trying to read the blank expression on the young man's face. Something had gone out of John that day, he knew. But something else had gone into him, as well. Something dark and brooding, distant and unfathomable, as if he were holding in a tremendous amount of anger that could burst forth in a rage at any moment.

"You're not thinking of going after those men, are you, John?" Ben said. He drove a stake into the ground, slipped a tent loop over it, stretching the fabric taut.

"Soon as we eat, I'm going to saddle up Gent and get on the trail of those killers."

"You going to ride your daddy's horse?"

"Why not? It's mine now, I reckon."

"Yeah, I reckon it is. Thought you might take Blue Boy since he knows you."

Blue Boy was a blue roan that had been John's horse. He liked the horse, but Gent was a distance horse, a Missouri-bred trotter that was as easy to ride as sitting on a cushion in a rocking chair. Tall and rangy, the horse had three white stockings, a star blaze, and a mane and tail like fine black silk. Blue Boy was stocky, just a little over fourteen hands high and was like riding a peg-legged barrel over a bumpy road.

"Gent's got good bottom. He's a distance horse. Blue Boy spooks at every shadow, balks at every bridge or gate, and rides like he's got four wooden legs."

"You count how many there were, Johnny?"

"Eight."

"Yep. Eight hard men. Every damned one of them a crack shot. You want to commit suicide?"

"I want those bastards to pay."

"Never knew you to curse, John."

"That's not cursing, Ben. That's what they are. Bastards. Every damned one of them."

"Whoa up, boy. Don't get your dander up. I'm not saying they ain't bastards. I'm just saying, you can't rightly go up against eight armed men all by your lonesome."

"I don't mean to," John said.

"You like to explain that, Johnny?"

"Once I get on their track, I'll hunt them down like a flock of turkeys. Scatter them. Pick 'em off one by one."

"How you going to manage that?"

"Call 'em out, one by one. Like scraping a turkey call. One comes at me, I blow his brains out. The others will likely run and I'll be on them like ugly on an ape. Call me another, and then another and another until every one of them is worm meat."

"I never heard you talk in such a way, Johnny. You scare the living hell out of me." Ben moved to the next stake, drove it, at a slant, into the ground, hooked it with a loop.

"I'll light the fire," John said and walked away.

"God, he even walks different," Ben said under his breath. It seemed to him that John had grown taller, his back had gotten straighter, as if he had iron in it, and he was no longer the gangly awkward kid with peach fuzz on his face. John had been shaving once a month, but his beard was soft and light, like down, and it was hard to tell whether he had shaved or not half the time.

Ben finished with the tent and began collecting pots and pans, searching through the detritus for food he might cook. He filled the coffeepot and put it on the fire to boil, then scooped ground coffee beans into it. He put some fatback in a fry pan, and set that on the stones next to the fire John had made. He mixed flour and water in a bowl, salted it slightly and formed the dough into lumps. He greased another fry pan, ladling spoonfuls of lard into the pan after it had heated, watched the lumps of lard skitter like some sentient beings, until they all melted. Then he dropped the doughballs into the pan. The grease sizzled in both frypans, and the coffee began to boil, spewing aromatic vapors from its spout.

"I'm going to dig it up," John said enigmatically.

"Huh?"

"My strongbox."

"Oh," Ben said. He watched John pace off a distance from where his tent had been to a spot beneath where his uncle's tent had been pitched. He picked up a spade and began to dig.

Some of the white clouds began to develop dark gray underbellies, and they continued to push up from some far valley in the mountains, clearing the visible snowcapped peaks and spreading out. The air felt different now, slightly cooler and heavier than before, as if the clouds were pushing it down with some invisible force or weight. Ben sniffed the vagrant breeze that wafted down from the mountains and stirred the coals and made the flames whip and dance like a kind of fluttering dervish that lasted only a few moments. He shivered involuntarily, as if cold drops of water had trickled down his back.

"Gonna storm, Johnny," Ben called, as John bent down and grabbed a box by the handle.

"Yeah, maybe. Why I want to get on the track of those murdering sonsofbitches while there's still tracks to read."

He gave a heave and grunted, pulling a large metal box from the hole in the ground. He carried it over to the fire and set it down in front of one of the logs. He sat down and fished in his pocket for a key.

"You got it locked and all," Ben said, reaching out for two tin cups. The fatback sizzled in the pan and the biscuits swelled.

He spooned hot grease onto the biscuits, turning their edges a silky brown.

"Damned right," John said, twisting the key in the lock. There was a clicking sound as the tumblers moved inside. John raised the top and reached inside. "Pa gave me this pistol and I aim to use it to avenge his death and all the others."

"You ain't no killer, John," Ben said softly.

Ben's eyes widened as John pulled out a rolled-up oilcloth with something heavy inside. John carefully unfolded the cloth and reached down, lifting the pistol by its butt.

"That's the pistol your daddy give you?" Ben said, scooting over closer to John for a better look.

"Yeah. On my last birthday. My legs gave out when I saw it."

"I seen your daddy's Colt before. But not like that."

"When we went to Santa Fe that time, Daddy said he had it done there. Isn't it beautiful?"

The pistol was truly beautiful, with fine scrollwork on the barrel that was inlaid with silver. On it were some words inscribed in Spanish.

"Just hold it right there, Johnny, whilst I pour the coffee. That's some pistol. I never saw one like it."

Ben poured the coffee into the two cups. He handed one to John, who set it down on the ground. He laid the oilcloth on a smooth spot, then set the pistol down, displaying it for both of them to see. He picked up his cup, blew away the cobwebs of steam, and sipped.

Ben scooted still closer after he pulled the fry pans further away from the direct flames of the fire. He gazed at the pistol.

"Them pearl-handled grips?" he said.

John shook his head.

"Ivory. Pure African ivory. Daddy had those hand carved in Santa Fe, too. A silversmith done the scrolling and the inlays. Tasco silver, Daddy said."

"What are them words written there? I can't see 'em right well, but they look like they're in a foreign language."

"Spanish," John said. "When you give me Lee's holster, they'll have more meaning, I reckon."

"You know what they mean?"

"Uh-huh. Daddy told me, and I learned some Mexican while we were in Santa Fe."

A cloud of small brown birds wheeled in the sky, all twittering on the wing. They flew in circles as if they were being chased, then darted in perfect synchronization up the side of the mountain and disappeared into the pines.

"Birds," Ben said. "Antic before a storm."

"What does that mean?" John asked.

"Just an old weather saying, I reckon. I think it's from literature. A poem, maybe. When birds fly like that, crazy as bedbugs, it means there's a whopping big storm coming. You can almost feel it now. Look at them underbellies on those big, white clouds. That's rain, Johnny. Getting ready to fall."

John looked up. The sky was indeed darkening and the breeze was stiffening, making the fire flap like clothes on a line in a high wind. The smell of flour baking and the aroma of bacon wafted to their nostrils. John felt his stomach churn with hunger and he took another sip from his cup.

"Yeah, it's going to rain like a cow pissing on a flat rock," John said.

"Where'd you ever hear that?"

"From Pa, I reckon." He jiggled his shoulders and arms. "Getting colder, too."

"That it is, Johnny. Now about them words on the barrel of that Colt."

"There are two lines, Ben. One on the left side, where you're looking, and another on the other side."

John lifted the pistol, turned it over. He held it close to Ben's face so he could see, but he didn't give the pistol to him. Nor did Ben make a move to touch it or take it from John's hand.

"This side," John said, pointing to the left side of the barrel, "reads, *'Ni me saques sin razon.'* And, on the other side, it says, *'Ni me guardes sin honor.'*"

"You speak Mexican right good, Johnny."

"Well, it's Mexican, all right. But, it's really Spanish, too, I reckon."

"And, you know what it means?"

For the first time that day, John smiled. It wasn't a big smile. He didn't show his teeth. But his mouth bent and there was a twinkle in his eye. Ben decided that it was a smile.

From some high meadow far above them, a bull elk bugled. The notes rose to a high, shrill pitch, then spiraled back down into the low notes, ending in a grunt. The call echoed off rimrock, carrying a long way, then died out softly in the smothering density of the muffling pine forest.

"He's marking his territory," Ben said. "A mite too early to be courting the ladies."

"Sounds like a big one," John said, his head cocked to hear the last dying notes of the plaintive call.

"He'll have him a set of horns come summer's end."

The clouds seemed to lower in the sky and

those above them and to the north were growing darker, the blackness underneath seeping up on the sides, like malevolent shadows. They had not yet heard any thunder, but these were the kinds of clouds that carried that threat in their billowing folds of condensed moisture.

"You want to know what the words mean?" John asked.

"I would, Johnny. I truly would."

"They mean this: 'Do not draw me without reason, nor keep me without honor.' "

"Why, that's right purty," Ben said. "I never heard nothin' like it, I reckon."

"It almost gives a life to the gun, doesn't it, Ben?"

"I don't know. Maybe. Depends on what you mean."

"As if the gun had a mind and is telling its owner how to behave, how to act, you know?"

"Yeah, I reckon that's kind of what the words mean, all right."

"That's what they mean. And I intend to obey them."

"Meaning you won't draw your pistol without having a damned good reason, eh?"

"Yeah. And because my father gave it to me, I'll keep it with honor."

Ben took another sip of coffee.

"I reckon you will, Johnny. It's the other part I'm worried about."

"What?"

"About not drawing less'n you got good reason."

"Oh, when I draw it, Ben, I'll have good reason. You can damned well bet on that, Mr. Russell."

The smile was gone, if it had ever been on John's face. Instead, his visage seemed to darken like the clouds, and Ben sensed there was thunder and lightning inside of him, just waiting, like a fuse, to be touched off.

And the afternoon was coming on, like the brewing storm, when the two men finally ate without much talk between them. Later, Ben found his brother Lee's holster and gave it to John.

John strapped it on. The belt bristled with .45-caliber cartridges. John slid the pistol inside the holster and it was a perfect fit. He wore the gunbelt well, as if he were born with it, and it born to decorate him. When he stood up and drew the pistol so fast his hands were a blur, like the downward plunge of a hawk, Ben felt that icy water creep back up his spine. He had never seen anything so fast. Until John drew a second time.

"Just practicing, Ben," he said.

"I reckon that's a reason."

They both knew what Ben meant. The trouble was that Ben didn't know what John was practicing the fast draw for. At least he didn't for sure.

But he had a pretty good idea.

The clouds began to darken and thicken, and far off there was the murmur of thunder, so soft they almost missed hearing it. The wind turned brisk and the air was thick with the smell of rain, rain that was, just then, only a promise, not a threat.

Just like Johnny Savage, Ben thought as he put out the fire, using the spade to shovel sand and water on it, to bury it beyond redemption. They would not light another that day, nor for days to come. And their fare for tomorrow and many days hence most likely would be hardtack and deer jerky unless Ben missed his guess about John's plans.

John hadn't said a word, but Ben was getting to read him pretty well.

That pistol spoke volumes, even when it was sleeping in its holster, with those words emblazoned on its barrel. That pistol, Dan Savage's gun, was like a coiled snake, ready to strike the minute it sensed the heat of its prey.

That Savage gun.

8

There was something bothering Oliver Hobart as he and his men rode through the trees back toward their abandoned camp, which was now a prearranged rendezvous site. The creak of his saddle set off an insistent tattoo in his mind, so intrusive after the previous excitement, that he felt as if he had missed something important back at that mining camp. In the heat of battle, and the finding of the gold, the noise of the guns, there had been something else he should have seen back there.

But he didn't know what it was.

Not yet.

"Slow down, Red," he called to the man ahead of him, who was leading the pack of them through the forest.

"Huh?" Red turned his head to look back at Ollie.

"No damned need to wear out the horses. We got a long ride ahead of us yet."

"Oh, yeah." Red slowed his horse as Ollie raised his hand for the others to see.

"To a walk, Red," Ollie said.

All of the men slowed and the saddle creak shifted keys, lost its former rhythm. Now it was just a steady drone in Hobart's ear, more like the sound pond frogs made just after dusk.

A mule deer arose from its bed at the sound of the passing horses, its ears thrust forward, coned to catch and decipher the crackle of twigs, the pad of iron hooves. Its black tail twitched nervously as it stood above the dust wallow where it had lain since early morning. It resembled a large mouse with its oversized ears and gray coat. The doe lifted its head, its black nostrils poised to sniff and suction every vagrant scrap of scent that wafted its way. Through the trees it could see the legs of the passing animals, and it could smell the leather and the sweat, the horse scent and the man scent. But it held its rigid stance, tail flicking like a cat's in convulsive, jerky vibrations that were the only sign of its nervousness. The horses passed and their hoofbeats faded. It sniffed the wallow as if to mark its contours. Then it folded its forelegs and let its rump descend as it took back to its cool, soft bed in the pines.

Had Hobart seen the deer, he might have shot it. Not for food, but just for sport, just to satisfy that inner bloodlust, that fascination with death that he had owned since he was a boy with strange, compelling urges that he could not explain, but thought were normal. He killed his first cat when he was four years old, a kitten, actually, squeezing its neck with his tiny hands, shutting off its airway. He had watched it squirm and wriggle in his grasp, try desperately to escape its death. But he had mashed its throat with his thumbs, squeezing, squeezing until it grew feeble and its hind legs stopped clawing at his arms. He squeezed its neck until all movement stopped and felt a surge of heat in his veins, a satisfying drum throb at his temples, an exhilaratingly fast tempo to his heartbeat. A feeling of warmth and satisfaction suffused him. He had never forgotten that first thrill when he had taken life, nor had he since denied that lust to kill when it came over him.

Ollie never regretted killing anything, not the cats, the dogs, the birds, the wild game, and when he was almost at maturity, a girl who had called him a name for making unwanted advances. He had picked up a rock and smashed her head, thrilling to the massive amount of blood that poured from a scalp wound and trickled down her face. He had smashed her again and again, delighting in the crunching sound of her skull as it caved in, the ooze of her brains into her long yellow hair, and the glassy look in her eyes when she finally breathed her last.

Ollie added torture to his list of experiments on human beings. He tied hapless victims up, burned them with matches and cigarettes, choked them with water poured down their throats, cut them with knives so that they slowly bled to death, affording him an opportunity to observe their final moments, to exult in his power over life and death. Hobart practiced his cruelty and when he could handle a gun, he took pleasure in ending a man's life in that manner. Shooting a man to death had its own rewards. As long as he could see the light fade from his eyes, in a single second, an hour, or a day, he drew satisfaction from the killing.

And Hobart had never been caught.

They halted their horses in the clearing where they had camped before raiding the miners on the creek. The horses snorted and blew, whinnied as they recognized a former home.

"Give the gold sacks to me, Red," Ollie

said. "I'll keep them until we get to Pueblo."

"Can't we divide it up now?" Fritz asked. "I mean, we got it and we're all here."

"No. We'll cash in the dust in Pueblo, like we planned," Ollie said. "Then we'll split up the money."

"Aw, shit," Pete Rutter complained.

"Yeah, let's do it now," Luke Wilkins growled, his eyes lit with a feral glow.

"Shut up, all of you," Ollie said, and his voice carried an authority that froze the men in their saddles. "What I say goes. Anybody who doesn't like it can light a shuck. But you'll go away without any dust in your poke. I mean it."

Ollie's hand rested on the butt of his pistol. And every man there knew that none of their company could beat him to the draw.

"Anybody?" Ollie said, meeting each man's gaze with his own steely stare.

"Hell, no, Ollie. That was the agreement," Pete said. "I just got the itch is all."

"Well, scratch in Pueblo, Pete."

The others laughed.

Ollie nudged his horse against Red's, held out his left hand.

"Let's have it, Red. You, too, Mort. Empty your saddlebags."

The two men dug in their saddlebags,

hefted the sacks of gold. Red handed his over, a sack at a time. Ollie slid them into one of his saddlebags, then the other, for balance.

"A goodly sum, I'd say." Ollie gave a smirk that might have passed for a smile, were it not for the look in his pale, cold eyes, like the eyes of an albino shark, as vacant of meaning or warmth as the glass eyes of a doll.

Mort made a show of dusting his hands after he handed over the last sack to Ollie. His horse lifted its tail slightly and blurted a blast of warm methane gas that spoiled the air with its rank stench. The fart rippled for a good five or six seconds.

"Was that a comment from you, Mort?" Ollie said, mirthlessly.

"No, sir. Mine don't make no noise. And they don't make no smell, neither."

Everyone laughed, except Ollie.

"That was a triple," Mandrake said, jokingly. "Whoo-weee. It do fairly stink. What you been feedin' that horse, Mort? Frijole beans?"

Again, everyone chuckled, except Ollie. As if he were judging them, checking to see if their mirth was genuine. Or if any of them had any regrets about what they had done and what his orders were.

A Canadian jay, pale as a ghost, landed on a laurel bush several yards away. Its faded blue feathers looked almost gray. Its tail feathers went into a spasm as it cocked it head and eyed something on the ground. Ollie saw it and wished he had a scattergun in his hands. The jay, as if sensing his intentions, hopped into the air and flapped away like some ghost bird dusted by blowing snow from one of the high white peaks in the distance, where clouds soared over them like a silent cotton explosion.

Ollie fixed Luke with a stare that was as hard and cold as the snout of a bullet.

"Something I don't like about that mess back there," Hobart said. "Luke, you and Pete were the lookouts."

"Yeah," Luke said. "So what?" His eyes shifted in their sockets. He knew he was almost as fast on the draw as Ollie. And he was a mite faster than anybody else. But, though he was bristling, he knew how long a split second was, and he didn't like the odds. Ollie looked ready to cut bait, for sure.

"Something I didn't like there. Can't put my finger on it real quick, but I want to go over it. With all of you."

"Yeah, well, go ahead with it then," Mandrake said, a veiled belligerence in his tone. "Pueblo's a long damned way, Ollie."

"All right. How many people did we count a day ago? Two days ago? Luke?"

Luke glared at Ollie, those little pig eyes of his just catching enough sun to spark like struck flint.

"I don't know. A dozen, I reckon."

"Well, think. Pete?"

"Yeah, a dozen, Ollie."

"Anybody count how many we rubbed out?"

Ollie's gaze swept the assemblage.

"I counted eleven, countin' the woman and the little gal. I mean, you got to count them, don't you?"

"You counted eleven," Ollie said, with a sarcastic twang. "Christ, Mort. How many did we count when we first started lookin' that camp over?"

Pete held up his hand and started touching the tips of his fingers.

"I know we counted 'em, Luke," he said. "Me and you."

"Yeah, we counted 'em for two days straight, at least."

"And how many people were there, men, women, and kids?" Ollie asked.

Pete touched ten fingers, then another three.

"That's an unlucky number," Pete said, as if dumbstruck by his venture into mathematics.

"What's an unlucky number?" Luke asked, irritation in his voice.

"Thirteen, Luke. We counted thirteen. Right?"

"If you say so, Pete." Luke's eyes glittered like bright beads caught in sunlight. He avoided looking at Hobart, whose right hand had fallen to his pistol holster almost as if trained to do that when not otherwise occupied. It was not a threatening gesture, but with Ollie's massive and formidable shape and size, almost any movement he made put people on guard.

"So, thirteen people were mining that stretch of creek, and we killed, what? Eleven of them. What happened to the other two, Pete? Luke?"

Pete shrugged and dipped his head like some penitent.

Luke tossed his head to one side, a gesture that had much the same meaning as a shrug.

"Did any of you see those stairs up the side of that little bluff in back of their camp?" Ollie asked.

Three or four of the men nodded.

"What else did you see or hear this morning, Luke, when you and Pete were glassing those folks?"

"I heard what sounded like an explosion,"

Pete said. "And we saw some smoke up yonder, where them steps was."

"That right, Luke?" Ollie's tone sounded almost casual.

"I guess we heard kind of a whumpin' sound," Luke said. "I thought it might have been thunder way off."

"Did you see smoke? Dust? Hear any rocks falling?"

"I seen some smoke, maybe," Luke said.

"Well, there are two of them pilgrims didn't make it to boot hill," Ollie said, his right hand flexing open and closed as if he were limbering it up.

Mort's horse bleated a short burst of flatulence, then lifted its tail and began ejecting apples from its rectum. The misshapen brown balls fell in a pile, along with green scum, making a series of wet plops as they struck the ground and each other.

"Mort, maybe you ought to take that nag to a privy somewheres," Army Mandrake said, "before he pisses all over us."

Nobody laughed. They were all thinking of that explosion, trying to decipher not only what it meant, but what Ollie thought it meant.

"So," Ollie said, "we got a couple of hard-rock miners in that bunch. And we missed 'em. They're still back there. Alive, goddamnit. And maybe them two saw our faces."

"That ain't likely," Luke said.

"Oh, what makes you say that, Luke?" Ollie said.

"Well, nobody shot at us. We didn't see nobody else. Everybody what was there eatin' grub got rubbed out, slicker than snot."

"Well, maybe they were scared shitless," Ollie said. "Maybe they didn't have any guns. But there's damned sure a mine up above that little bluff and them two bastards had to hear us come barreling in there shooting off our guns like we was a county fair."

None of the men said a word.

Ollie let the silence settle in before he broke it.

"All right," Hobart said. "Here's what we're going to do." He looked at Luke and Pete. His glance was withering, as if his eyes could project heat and melt stone or wilt grass. "Luke, you and Pete are going back there and finish the job."

"What?" Luke said. "Go back there? Hell, we need to go to Pueblo with you to get our cut."

"We'll wait for you."

"Shit," Luke said.

"You two ride back and clean up any mess

you see. I want proof. Cut their scalps off or their balls, but I want them two men dead and gone by the time you get to Pueblo. If you don't show up, we'll all say a prayer for your sorry asses."

"Damn, Ollie," Pete said. "Why don't we just let it be? Or else all of us go back and see if there's anybody there?"

"Pete, this discussion is over. Now git, the both of you. And, remember, I want proof. I don't want to spend the rest of my days lookin' over my shoulder wondering if them two jaspers are traipsin' after us."

Grumbling under his breath, Luke clucked to his horse and dug spurs into its flanks. Pete spurred his horse and followed after him. The two men vanished into the woods, the brush rustling, small limbs snapping as they went.

"Let's go to Pueblo, boys," Ollie said.

"What if they don't come back?" Dick Tanner said.

"Then, we'd sure as hell better watch our backs, Dick," Ollie said, slapping his horse on the rump with his reins. The others fell in beside Ollie. One or two of them looked back as they rode away.

Clouds darkened the land as the men turned south and east, heading toward Fountain Creek. They cast no shadows and the caw of a crow as it flapped overhead was the only sound they heard.

Ollie hoped Luke and Pete would join them in Pueblo. In fact, he was counting on it. If they had left two men alive back there, these boys were both crack shots.

He just hoped they had more wits than they'd had that morning.

Ollie didn't want anybody on his backtrail bent on revenge.

And he sure as hell didn't want those two miners going to the law.

More crows flew overhead, cawing noisily as they flapped toward the long prairie beyond the mountains. They were specks in the sky by the time Ollie stopped thinking about the two nameless miners who were still alive and witnesses to nearly a dozen cold-blooded murders.

9

With mumbles of thunder in the distance, Ben and John quickly picked up the campground, carried all the items into the pitched tent. The sky had turned from a slate gray to an obsidian black, with huge thunderheads sinking lower, blotting out the snow-capped peaks, replacing the murky creek waters with lampblack.

"I'd better get going, Ben," John said. "I want to get a look at those tracks. You can finish up here. I'll see you again, someday."

John stuck out his hand.

"Johnny," Ben said, "put your hand down. I'm going with you."

"No, Ben. You can't."

"Yes, I can. And I am."

"You don't know what you're getting into, Ben."

"Neither do you. But if you think I'm going to batch it here in this camp all by myself, you've got another think coming.

Besides, you're outmanned and outgunned. I'm going with you and no damned argument."

"Well, that's good of you. I just think I ought to go at this alone."

"We've been partners here, haven't we? Why break it up, Johnny? I've got my Yellow Boy and a Colt pistol and I can shoot the eye out of a gnat at twenty-five yards."

"I could do without the bullshit, Ben. Let's go, then. But, don't say I didn't warn you. Neither of us might ever get back here."

"You could use another set of eyes and ears, though. Am I right?"

"Ben, it'll be a pleasure."

It was settled then. The two walked in long, ground-eating strides up the road to the barn. They carried their rifles, cartridges, sacks of jerky, tins of peaches and apricots. John's knife hung from his belt, snug against his hip. Each of them wore two shirts and two pairs of pants for a change of clothing, and they had balled-up socks in their back pockets.

"What are you going to do about the horses and mules?" Ben asked.

"Take off their hobbles and turn 'em out," John said. "Leave the barn open. There's hay and grain in there and if they have good sense, come winter, they'll come in out of the cold."

"Good idea. I'll get two halters, catch up my little gelding, Dynamite, and fetch Gent. You lay out the saddles, bridles, and blankets. I'll take the hobbles off the others."

A mule deer bounded up into the center of the meadow, trotted toward the far trees on the opposite side, a shadow against the dull green of the field and trees, its black tail twitching in silent warning. One of the horses whickered and a mule gave an answering bray. John went into the barn, opened the tack room door, and laid out saddles, bridles, blankets, and saddlebags. He found a scabbard for his Winchester and took Ben's down from a dowel driven into the log wall.

It was dark inside the barn, the only light a few gray shafts spearing the heavy shadows like mystical lances. A column of dull light stood in the doorway like a block of transparent rock, its rectangular shape filled with fluttering motes that danced like phantom fireflies.

John carried the gear outside and set it down. Ben had taken the hobbles off several horses and was kneeling down in front of another. The meadow was bathed in an odd twilight, the black clouds so low they obscured the tops of the tall trees, hid the mountains. The grass had a metallic cast to it, a strange hue that seemed to break up the spectrum, imparting a dull yellow and blue mixed in with the hard dark green. The spindly trunks of aspens along the small creek shivered in the wind, bone white against the brown backdrop of pines.

Ben put halters on his mottled gray gelding and John's black Gent, started leading them toward the barn. Some of the horses followed at a distance, their manes tousled by the wind, shaking across their necks like swaying tassels on a lampshade.

"Here's your Gent," Ben said, handing the halter reins to John.

The two men slapped blankets on the backs of their horses, hefted single-cinched Denver saddles, snugged them on the blankets, pulled the straps underneath the horses' bellies, and secured the cinches through O-rings. They attached their rifle sheaths, draped their saddlebags behind the cantles, filled them with ammunition and grub sacks. Last, they folded and bundled their rain slickers and tied them on with leather thongs attached to the saddles just behind the cantles.

Both men looked up at the black whales of clouds swimming just over their heads, great bulging masses that seemed to be growing larger by the minute. They mounted up as the horses in the field stood like statues watching them go.

Thunder grumbled in the distance and the wind swirled and surged from different directions, circling, sniffing like an invisible wolf through their shirts and at their hair, ruffling their hats, surging through the grasses and bending the stems of wildflowers that had closed their petals as if for night in the waning hours of a blackening afternoon.

Ben noticed that John did not even look at their camp as they approached. He didn't look at the tent Ben had pitched, nor at any of the familiar landmarks. Instead, he headed straight for the creek, entering it almost at the same point the killers had, when they rode off into the woods following the massacre.

The creek waters boiled. Little bubble nests of soapsuds scudded out from the shadows of rocks that poked their heads out, creating small eddies amid the sudsy turbulence. It seemed to be running fuller and swifter, as though, higher up, rain had already begun to fall. As if to underscore Ben's thoughts, there were muffled grunts of thunder from the north, sounding like the guttural groans of some great leviathan approaching on rolling combers across a great, turbulent sea. And the wind grew colder, snapping at them with lusty gusts, licking their faces with icy tongues, lashing their earlobes until they turned pink as if stung by bees.

As soon as they entered the trees, John bent his head and looked down at the ground. Ben knew that he was seeing the same things he was, a maze of horse tracks, ground churned up by iron hooves, the plain track of men fleeing a scene of carnage on horseback.

John's blood quickened when he saw the tracks. He did not try to count them. He knew how many men had come to kill. He knew their faces. He knew the names of some. It was warmer now that they were in the trees. He rubbed the sting of cold from his left earlobe, then shifted hands and warmed the other. The storm was still far off. He had heard no thundercrack, nor seen any flash of light in the dark and ponderous sky. But he knew it was coming and was glad they had their slickers and were wearing extra shirts.

The horse tracks were dark scars on the land, difficult to see in the mingled shadows of the thick pines. But the outlaw horses had been running and their hooves tore through fallen pine needles, dislodged small stones, plowed soft earth, so that they left a wide swath that John could follow. The heady scent of loam and the musty fragrance of the pines conjured up memories of his Arkansas home, his father and mother. His little sister.

Dan Savage had come to the Ozarks from Knoxville, Tennessee, with his parents, Obie and Belinda Savage, a few years after the War Between the States. Dan had met Clare shortly after that and married her. They had taken up farming in Jasper, south of Harrison. John remembered growing up along the Buffalo River, hunting deer in the hardwoods on soft hills that blazed with every color of the rainbow in fall. The two of them hunted squirrels with small-caliber black powder rifles, .36-caliber single-shot muzzleloaders. They caught catfish and bass on cane poles near late-night campfires and hiked the hills and hollows in search of morels every redbud- and dogwood-blooming spring. His mother would soak them in salty water to clear out all the dirt, soak them in milk, and simmer them in a hot skillet. They ate wild poke and collard greens, black-eyed peas, and hog jowls every New Year's Day, and celebrated Christmas with a lighted cedar tree.

The memories flooded through John's mind until he felt a sharp blow to his right shoulder. He turned in anger and saw Ben riding right next to him. Ben held a single finger to his mouth, then flattened his hand in a signal to stop.

John reined in Gent and looked quizzically at Ben. He opened his mouth to speak, but again, Ben held a finger to his lips, indicating silence. Then he pointed to his ear, cupped it.

John turned his head, trying to pick up whatever sound Ben had heard, or thought he had heard. He looked at Gent's ears. They were stiffened into taut cones and twisted first one way, then another.

A silence rose up around them.

John waited. Listened.

Then, he heard it. Off to his left, a furtive sound, unnatural. A footstep? A small sound, like a foot touching pine needles and earth, then a scraping sound as if someone had brushed against the bark of a pine tree.

A second or two later, he heard another sound, this one off to his right. He looked at Ben.

Ben held up two fingers.

He pointed left and then right. And again, he held up two fingers.

John nodded.

Ben was telling him there were at least two men making those noises. Not deer. Not elk. Not squirrels or chipmunks. Men. Hiding, or waiting in ambush.

Ben put a finger to his lips again, then drew his rifle very slowly from its sheath. He pointed down, then, in slow motion, drew his left foot from the stirrup and raised it. His saddle creaked when he shifted all of his weight to his right foot, swung his left leg over the saddle. He eased himself to the ground, left his reins trailing.

John did the same. He carefully slipped his rifle from its sheath, his body tensed for any sound he might make. He left the saddle in the same slow way as Ben. He stepped around Ben's horse until he stood next to him.

Ben pointed to his chest, then motioned to the right.

John nodded, then signed that he would go left.

Then Ben bent his head and put his mouth close to John's ear.

"Stand behind a tree and wait," Ben whispered.

John nodded, breath streaming through his nostrils, slow and quiet.

He walked to a tree, taking his time, setting his feet down, finding firm footing, then advancing the other foot. He got behind a pine tree and held his rifle pointed upward, his thumb on the hammer. He had already levered a cartridge into the firing chamber and the hammer was on half cock.

There was another short silence before John heard anything else. A very small twig crackled. Hardly noticeable, but enough to jangle John's nerves and sound warning klaxons in his brain.

He heard a quick shuffle, as if someone had dashed from one tree to the next. He peered around the tree, trying to see movement in the gloom of the cloudy day, the heavy shadows of the trees.

A quail piped a short whistle. That was off to his right. Only John knew it was not a quail. There was an answering call to his left. Then another scurry of feet, and he saw movement. It took him a second or two to realize that he had seen the figure of a man, advancing toward him on foot. The man carried a weapon of some sort. Either a rifle or shotgun. He couldn't be sure.

He looked behind him, but saw only his and Ben's horses. There was no sign of Ben.

Were there only two men?

John wondered.

Had they ridden into an ambush? Were all eight killers just waiting to shoot them to ribbons?

The seconds crawled by, like small eternities stretching into a dark infinity.

The waiting was agony for John.

He pulled his head back, but kept the image of where he had seen the man locked tight in his mind. He wondered how he could draw the man into the open, turn the tables on him and surprise him. He knew there would only be a split second to aim and fire his rifle. And, if there were any small branches between him and his target, the bullet could deflect and miss its mark. That had happened to him more than once when hunting deer. He had been forced to learn to see not only the deer, but all the space between the animal and the muzzle of his rifle.

There was another slight sound a few yards in front of him. The man had scraped his shoulder or his leg against a tree. That's what it had sounded like, John thought.

He drew a shallow breath, held it. His thumb worried the scored top of the hammer. He slid down the length of the tree until he was squatting. His knees jutted out, as did part of his rump. But he figured the man would be looking for him to be standing up, and might not look toward the ground at all.

John nearly jumped out of his skin as he heard a loud explosion off to his right. The sound was one he knew. Ben's Henry had spoken and the noise was deafening.

He heard a muffled shout and peered from behind the tree, looking up to where he had last seen the man heading toward him.

"Pete," the man called, and John saw him step out from behind a tree.

He knew that face, even in the murky light; John knew that one of the killers was standing less than twenty-five yards from him, his body partially concealed by brush, but his head tilted upward. His face clearly visible.

Something came unwound inside John. He squeezed the forestock of his rifle. He pulled gently on the trigger as he pushed the hammer back, cocking the rifle, making only a small sound as the action engaged.

One shot. That's probably all he would get, John thought.

His brain raced with images, the jumbled formula of a plan that could get him killed. In between the layers of thought, a scratching of a warning finger, a small word of caution unspoken, but understood.

A rifle cracked and he heard the whine of a bullet as it caromed off a solid object.

Then, the heavy *boom* of the Henry again and this time he heard its echoes before the sound died away.

John made his decision.

He took another breath, then rolled away from the tree, throwing himself headlong on the ground. He found himself plunged into an alien world where dragons spewed flame and nightmares came into being out of some cavernous dungeon deep in the recesses of his mind. Two explosions shattered the taut silence in his brain.

In that first instant, when he was exposed, lying flat on the ground, putting the butt of his rifle to his shoulder, a giant pair of iron doors swung wide open.

His blood froze.

The gates of Hell opened.

Fire and brimstone rained down on him.

10

Luke Wilkins touched off both triggers. His double-barreled shotgun roared, spewing bright orange flame and buckshot straight at the tree where John had been standing moments before. Lead sprayed a hailstorm of death in a six-foot-wide pattern. The balls ripped through pine bark, tore needles and branches from the tree, ripped through the underbrush, scything foliage into shreds.

John fired his Winchester, aiming straight at the twin flowers of flame. He dropped his rifle and rolled to the left, snatching his Colt from his holster, cocking the single-action weapon as it cleared the holster. He heard the deadly thrash of shot shearing through the brush, the smack of lead balls against tree trunks.

He saw the shotgunner stagger into the lingering cloud of smoke. He jumped to his feet before the man could reload and charged toward him. The man dropped his shotgun and clawed for his pistol, a blue-black hole in his left leg, near the groin.

John stopped and fired his Colt, aiming for the man's heart. But Luke's left leg gave way and tilted him sideways, so the bullet from John's gun struck his right shoulder, spun him like a top. His pistol slipped from his hand. John hammered back and took two steps, fired point-blank at the man's belt buckle. He heard the sickening slap of the bullet as it struck flesh square in the man's bellybutton, caving his midsection in, collapsing him like a man performing knee bends. The man sagged and pitched forward with a grunt of pain, blood spilling from his gut, jetting from his shoulder in measured, heart-pumping bursts.

John ran to the man, slid a boot under his chest, and flipped him over. He cocked the Colt and shoved its snout forward until it butted up against the man's forehead. He reached down, jerked the man's pistol from its holster and tossed it out of reach.

"You're the one they call Luke," John said.

Luke batted his eyes. They were laced with pain. He held both hands over the hole in his belly and blood seeped through the spread fingers, painting his hands so that they resembled a white-and-crimson-striped fan.

"Where are the rest of them?" John barked.

"You don't kilt me," Luke said.

"Not yet, you bastard. Where are the others?"

"Gone," Luke croaked. "Help me."

"I'll help you, Luke. Just tell me where your friends went."

"Fountain," Luke said.

"Fountain Creek?"

"Yeah."

"Then where? Where do you meet them?"

"Fuck you," Luke said, his pig eyes narrowing under hooded lids.

"I'll help you, same as you helped my family, Luke," John said, his voice measured, low, menacing.

Luke's eyes opened wide. A spasm of pain coursed through his body. Both men could smell his ruptured intestines. The odor was as foul as a barnyard or a feedlot. The stench caused Luke to crinkle his nose and even that small movement made him wince in pain. His breathing became more labored. Blood spurted from his shoulder and leg wounds with every few beats of his heart. The color that suffused his face began to fade. His complexion turned to the color of dough. His lips began to turn slightly blue as he struggled to breathe.

"Shoot me," Luke begged. "Just go ahead and shoot me."

"Be merciful, eh?"

"Yeah."

"I want you to think about that little girl, Luke. My sister. And the woman. My mother. Think about them and all the others while you leak blood through your miserable guts. Think about the mercy you showed them, you pathetic sonofabitch."

"Ahhh," Luke breathed.

John raised his foot and ground the heel into Luke's crotch.

Luke screamed in agony.

There was a commotion in the brush off to John's right. Footsteps. He turned and swung his pistol toward the sounds.

Luke fixed his gaze on John's pistol, on the silver inlay, the ivory grips. His wet eyes widened, tried to focus as his life leaked slowly away.

Ben emerged from tree and cloud shadows, the receiver of his Yellow Boy gleaming like a miniature sunrise, as if he held a bar of freshly minted gold in his hand. His face was contorted in pain and he limped into full view.

"You hurt?" John's expression registered concern.

"Twisted my blamed ankle chasin' after

that other'n. He got clean away."

"I thought I heard someone yelling, like he was hurt."

"That could have been me. Could have been him. I think I nicked him."

"Get a good look at him?" John asked.

"No. He lit a shuck. Ran like a scared rabbit. I twisted my ankle and had to give up on him. What you got here?"

Ben looked down at Luke and swore under his breath.

"God, Johnny, what're you doing to him?"

"Waiting."

"Waiting for what?"

"He — he's waitin' for me to die, the bastard," Luke said, a malevolent glare in his narrowed eyes. "Torturin' me. You shoot me, mister. I'm done for."

Ben lifted his rifle.

John put a hand on the barrel and pushed it down.

"No," John said. "I'm going to tell Luke here about my family."

"What?" Ben said.

"Find yourself a seat under a tree. Get off that ankle."

Ben hobbled to a pine, rested against it, and slid to the ground. He laid the Henry across his lap, pushed his hat back off his forehead.

John squatted next to Luke, holding the pistol up so the wounded man could see it, see that it was cocked, see that his finger was just a breath away from the trigger.

"You killed my little sister, Luke. You or one of your ugly friends. She wasn't but ten years old. Her name was Alice. She had the prettiest hair, golden hair, like spun honey."

"I didn't kill that kid," Luke said.

"Shut up, Luke," John said amiably, his eyes glittering like the eyes of the mad, like the eyes of a predator watching its prey.

"She played with dolls, made up little stories about them, and she pretended that they were real people. They were her friends and she made tea for them and mudpies and fed them like a mother spoon-feeds a real baby."

"Don't," Luke said, a pleading note in his voice.

There was a sound like an empty barrel rolling across the floor of a cavernous room. Thunder rolling across the skies, the sound pushing through thick black clouds like an immense voice shouting through layers of cotton. And the sound died away, leaving a hush behind, and a darker darkness.

"She had the prettiest laugh, Luke. She said her dolls made her laugh. And she would draw pictures of them on paper and show her pictures to them, and sometimes it seemed so real, I thought her dolls were laughing with her. She found a little bird once, down in Arkansas, and it had a broken wing. She took that bird and put in a little box and told her dollies to help her take care of it. She put medicine on its wing and one of her dolls was a nurse and she had that little birdie hopping around in no time. That's how kind she was. That's how she treated God's creatures. When the bird got well and flew away, Alice just laughed and laughed, and she told her dolls how much they had helped that poor bird."

"Stop," Luke croaked. "No more. Please. I'm dyin'."

"Alice is already dead, Luke. She was shot to pieces by you and your men. I buried her with her favorite doll. They're both in the cold ground. And you ain't even goin' to get that, you miserable sonofabitch. You're going to feed the wolves and the worms."

Luke gasped for air. His eyes rolled wildly in their sockets.

Ben sat there, aghast at what John was doing.

None of them heard the man creeping up on them. Pete Rutter had heard the voices. He had circled around, slowly and carefully, so that he had a clear view of the three men.

Now he stared dumbstruck at the three of them through a pair of binoculars. He was close enough to hear what they were saying, but he knew he could not be seen. He watched and he listened.

Then he saw the pistol in John's hand. His jaw dropped as he focused the binoculars, brought the pistol up large enough to see the silver inlay, the image sharp in the lenses of his glasses.

He looked at Luke.

Blood dripped from Luke's shoulder and there was a large stain on his midsection, another on his leg. His face looked pale, his features threaded with pain.

He had seen enough. There was no saving Luke and he was outnumbered. One of the old fellow's bullets had struck his rifle, knocked the sights off. The young feller and the old guy were too far away for a pistol shot.

His heart pounding, Pete retreated, found his horse, and led him for some distance before he mounted him and stole away through the dark trees, heading toward Fountain Creek. Ollie would be mad as hell, but he wasn't going to stick around and face up to the young one. The one with the fancy pistol, the one who was torturing Luke and enjoying himself while Luke lay there, bleeding to death, his guts poking out of his abdomen like oily blue snakes.

Lightning flashed and there was a thundercrack that made four men jump inside their skins.

Thunder pealed across the sky and behind it the nattering whisper of rain, steaming down the mountainside, great sheets of it blown south and east by the wind.

"My mother, her name was Clare," John continued, "was the sweetest person I ever knew. She had a heart of gold and used to read stories to me at night. Even when she was tired from working all day, she'd tuck me and my sister Alice in bed every night and tell us stories until our eyelids got heavy and droopy and we fell asleep. She made my father Dan happy, too. And he doted on her. He treated her like a queen, and she treated him like a king. That was my mother, Luke, and she's lying in the ground, too, all of her stories dead on her lips."

"I can't take no more," Luke said. "Please don't tell me no more about them people."

"Them people, Luke? Why, you don't deserve to breathe the same air they did. You killed them. For what? Some gold that you'll spend on whores and whiskey? Buy yourself a new pair of boots, or a saddle? Spend money you didn't earn and took

from truly good people? People you murdered, you bastard."

"It was Ollie," Luke said. "He made us do
it."

"Ollie?"

"Hobart. He put us up to it."

"Well, I can't wait to meet Ollie Hobart,"
John said. "At the business end of this Colt
in my hand. I wonder how brave he's going
to be. As brave as you, you sniveling little
shit?"

"John, you done said enough," Ben said.

They could hear the rain now, off in the
distance, and there was lightning close by,
stitching jagged lines of silver in the black
clouds, striking the ground as thunderclaps
boomed in their ears and echoed through
the canyons, off the high rimrock, and off
into desolate nothingness.

The fissure in Luke's belly had widened
and coils of intestines were easing out. They
glistened like water snakes or nightcrawlers.
The hole in his abdomen had grown larger,
probably from the time John had put his
boot on his testicles, forcing Luke to react.

"Ben, bring up the horses and shake our
slickers, will you?" John said. "Can you
manage with that game ankle?"

"Yeah. I can manage." Ben got to his feet,
resting against the tree for support. "How

much longer you going to rag this poor bastard?"

"Just a while longer, Ben. Go on. That rain's going to hit us pretty quick."

"Yeah. I'll get the horses."

Ben hobbled off, using his rifle as a crutch.

"Luke, you still here?"

Luke had closed his eyes. His breathing was shallow and there were rales in it, as if his throat had filled with sand.

Luke opened his eyes.

"Yeah, you bastard." Raspy, weak, that was Luke's voice now. He had not long to live, John thought.

"I'll put you out of your misery if you tell me where Ollie and the others are going. Where they're going to hole up and wait for you."

"You won't do it."

"Yes, I will. One little squeeze of the trigger and your lamp goes out. Real quick. Real painless. Just tell me what I want to know and it'll be over just like that. You won't even feel the bullet."

"Christ."

"Yeah, you can pray, too, Luke. And go on suffering. I don't mind that. I'm suffering. Let me tell you about Pa, Dan Savage. We haven't got to him yet, but he was a man to ride the river with, Luke. Best father a boy could have. Hunted with him, fished with him, farmed with him, broke bread with him at my mother's fine table, with my little sister right by his side every night, adoring him as much as my mother did."

"No more, Savage."

"Oh, there's a lot more, Luke. There's my pa, and my uncle. Yeah, you killed him, too. And Ben's brother. Maybe he'll tell you about his brother, Leland; we called him Lee. A hell of a guy."

"Pueb . . ."

"What's that, Luke?"

"Pueblo," Luke gasped. "Ollie. Goin' to Pueblo."

"Ah, Pueblo. And, where in Pueblo were you going to meet him?"

"Can . . ."

"Can't hear you, Luke."

"Cantina."

"What's the name of the cantina, Luke? Hell, we're almost there. You won't have to bear the awful pain much longer. Just tell me the name of the cantina."

Luke convulsed as pain shot through his innards like molten fire. He sucked in a breath and the air stayed in his lungs a long time, as if it was never going to come out.

"Rosa," Luke growled, as if the sand in his throat had turned to gravel. "Rosa's

Cantina. On Calle Vaca. Now, do it, Savage. Do what you done promised."

Ben rode up, leading John's horse. Lightning swept the sky in jagged streaks, the thunder following almost immediately, a great roaring in the sky, a thousand cannons belching at once, cannonballs rolling across the hollow deck of a huge ship and fading into the distance, like the faint echoes of long-ago storms.

Ben had his slicker on, and he held John's in his hand.

"Here you go, John," Ben said. When John looked up, Ben tossed the wadded raincoat down at John. It landed next to him, in a crumpled heap, like a yellow bird fallen from the sky.

Luke groaned.

John picked up his slicker, stood up. He slid his arms through it and snugged it up.

"Now?" Luke said. "You goin' to send me on my way now, Savage? I done told you want you want to know."

John looked down at Luke. His face bore almost no expression.

"Do you know what penance is, Luke?"

"No. Just get it over with, will you?"

"Penance is the price you pay for your sins. That's what the preacher told us. Now, that's what you're going to do now. You're going to do penance."

John picked up Luke's pistol and tucked it inside his belt.

Then he climbed on his horse.

"You just going to leave him, Johnny?" Ben said.

"Yeah, Ben. I ain't no cold-blooded killer like old Luke there. I shot him in a fair fight, and that's as far as I'll go. This day, anyways."

"You know something, Johnny?"

"Something?"

"You got all the makings of a real bastard."

John turned Gent and began to ride away as the first stalks of rain speared through the pine branches, splattering on their slickers. A lightning flash splashed across Luke's face, a face frozen in terror. Rain spattered into his mouth and eyes and he tried to sit up. He stretched out a hand as if reaching for something. Something that was no longer there. Then he fell back. There was an ominous rattle in his throat and the breath he expelled was his last.

"You ain't got a bit of mercy in you, Johnny," Ben said as they rode away, heading east, away from the creek, away from all the deaths of that sullen and sorrowful day.

John said nothing. He knew he was not satisfied at all.

There were still seven killers left. Seven bad men still alive.

And, no, he thought, there was no mercy in him.

11

Ben pulled on the reins. Dynamite came to a halt. The dappled gray gelding whickered and tossed its head as raindrops needled its eyes. John stopped when Gent came up alongside.

"You want that shotgun, Johnny?" He pointed to the ground.

John looked down at Luke's scattergun.

"No, let it rust," he said.

"Perfectly good weapon. We might could use it."

Raindrops spattered on the twin barrels, the stock. Specks of bright red blood turned brown and ran off the metal and wood, swirling in lazy curlicues along the length of the barrel and stock. The sight reminded John of a time when he had cut his finger with a knife. His mother had held his hand over a white bowl and poured water on the wound. The blood had dripped into the bowl first, then the water had turned it brown as it diluted it. He had been fascinated by his own blood and the way the water had mixed with it, taken away its redness.

"It's got blood on it," John said.

"Yeah, that feller's blood."

"No. I mean different."

Ben nodded. "Yeah, maybe. What about that pistol you took offen him?"

"He didn't use it on our people. I might use it on his."

Ben shook his head and tapped Dynamite's flanks with his spurs. The horse stepped ahead and they rode through the rain.

"Still want to track them fellers?" Ben asked, raising his voice above the blowing rain.

"Yeah. I want to know as much about them as I can. Where they camped, for one thing."

"We'll pick up their trail."

John searched the ground for the remnants of tracks, and found them, the depressions filling up with water, but still visible.

"This must have been where they camped," Ben said, as lightning blistered the clouds with jagged bolts. The clearing lit up like a stage set and John saw the places where they had put their bedrolls, concave depressions in the earth. Their fire ring was black with ashes and charred wood. It was filling up with water, floating some of the burnt chips and splinters of firewood up to the surface.

Thoughts, a myriad of them, flooded John's brain as he scanned the camp. He knew the outlaws must have been there for more than a day or two. There was a smell to it now, as if the scents had been stirred up by the rain. He detected the odors of sweat and horsehair, of burnt wood and dead pine needles. And there was the musky scent of moss and the faint fragrance of blue spruce mingled with the pungent aroma of horse manure and urine, along with human offal. A feeling of disgust rose up in him that they had been so near, watching them, planning their hideous murders, breathing the same mountain air.

"How far, Ben? A mile or two from our camp?"

"Maybe that much. Hard to tell in this rain. I lost all landmarks when we got jumped back there."

"Too close, anyway."

"Yeah, Johnny. Too damned close."

"Let's follow the tracks out of here for as long as we can, then get out from under this damned rain."

"You find out anything from that Luke feller?"

"Yeah. Unless he was lying."

"Know where they're headed?"

"He said Pueblo."

"Makes sense. Cash in the dust and nuggets, light out north or south. Taos or Santa Fe. Colorado Springs, Denver. Cheyenne, maybe."

"Ever hear of a place called Rosa's Cantina?"

"Nope. I never heard of any cantina in Pueblo or anywhere else. You?"

"No. Luke said they were supposed to meet up there. It's on Calle Vaca."

"Sounds like he told you a lot."

"He didn't tell me enough, Ben."

"What do you mean?"

John slapped his horse on the rump with his reins and put the spurs to his tender flanks.

"He didn't say he was sorry."

The lightning stopped after a while, and the thunder faded in the distance. They rode through lashing rain, following pools of horse tracks, then even these vanished. Luckily, the wind-driven rain was at their backs as they angled through the range of mountains on a course for Fountain Creek.

They rode through curtains of liquid

crystal, following game trails that shed some water, giving their horses better footing, and through misty trees that muffled the sound of the wind-whipped rain that beat on their slickers like a thousand clocks ticking. Vapors arose from the floor of the forests, mists lingered in the groves of blue spruce and junipers and firs. Little rivers carved small gullies in the earth, and once they smelled bear scat and saw a juniper ripped by an elk's antlers. The wood was splintered and torn as if it had been struck by an exploding artillery shell, blasted to ruin by a rutting bull elk, in another autumn.

"We'll be stumblin' around in the dark here pretty quick," Ben said, just before dusk. The little daylight that was left was beginning to dim, shrinking away with every foot of gained ground.

"Yeah, I been looking for a place to hole up," John said. "We should have brought a tarp, so's we could make a lean-to."

"We can cut us a shelter with spruce branches," Ben said.

"Let's do it."

"We'll stay to high ground. Could be flash floods down in the bottoms of those canyons and ravines."

John nodded and they began to search for a suitable place to build a shelter. They were on a high ridge. They could feel the mountains around them, but could not see them. The wind howled and blew great sheets into them and across their path, cutting down their visibility. The wind made sounds in the trees and on the rimrock that sounded like the keening of lost souls, a shrieking that could drive a man to madness if it lasted long enough.

John knew how dangerous it was now. They could be following a trail that traversed a sheer drop on one or both sides. They could only see a few feet on either side. He looked for clumps of trees just off the trail. Raindrops stung his eyes when he looked, and from the whip of the wind, he knew they were exposed on some high ridge.

Ben spotted the trees as the trail descended. He pointed off to the right and turned his horse in that direction. John followed him, a lightness in his heart now that they were escaping the brunt of the wind and rain.

"Plenty of spruce and fir in here," Ben said as they rode into a grove of various-sized trees. They had passed a pair of stunted pines moments before, so knew that they had been on an exposed ridge, where the wind flattened their slickers against their backs and chests as it circled like a lion tamer cracking whips in an arena. The spruce trees were thick with branches and foliage, which shielded them from the brunt of the wind and knifing rain.

They tied the horses to small stunted pines where they were somewhat sheltered. Ben picked out a spruce tree and the two men began to shear off the lower branches, stacking them into two neat piles. Ben told John when to stop and they moved to the next spruce, trimming the lower limbs, and piling these up in separate piles. They left the top branches intact. They moved in a circle, trimming spruce trees, leaving a space among them for their bedrolls.

"Just watch what I do, Johnny, and you start on the other side. We're going to build walls, so's we can light us a fire, stay warm all night."

Ben began shoving spruce boughs against the trees, weaving them into those he placed at the base of the next tree. John did the same until they had a solid wall around the opening in the center. Ben had told John to use the short boughs for the walls. They then put the longer branches across the opening at the top, forming a dome. The needles acted like fringed leather on buckskin sleeves, allowing the water to drip off onto the ground using gravity. The top branches of the spruce which were still attached to the trunk gave them what amounted to several roofs over the one they had made with their hands. The walls were thick enough to withstand the wind and keep the top of the dome from caving in on them.

They stripped the horses of their saddles and saddlebags and the bedrolls, carrying them into the shelter through an opening Ben had left at the bottom of one side that could be closed when they were ready to go to sleep.

He and John collected small stones for the fire. It was pitch dark when they finished.

"Now, we get us some squaw wood for kindling," Ben said.

"What's that?"

"Follow me and I'll show you."

John followed Ben as he felt his way through the trees. Ben reached up and snatched the dry twigs that grew beneath the needled boughs. He stuffed these under his slicker.

"You'll find this dry wood at near every pine, Johnny. Now, don't get lost and I'll meet you back at the camp. We still need to find some decent deadwood for the fire."

John found plenty of squaw wood. The

small dead branches crackled when he broke them and brought them down. He made himself fat under his slicker and found his way back to the shelter. Ben had already placed his dry squaw wood in the center of the fire ring and had gathered some rotted wood from deadfalls.

"I hope there's more out there," Ben said. "We need to get enough wood to last the night."

"I stumbled over some downed logs out there," John said. "We'll do it."

In less than an hour, the two men had enough firewood, Ben figured, to last them through most of the night. It was still raining hard, but they were out of the wind inside their shelter. Ben struck a match and touched it to the squaw wood. Flames licked the dry branches. John piled more wood on as the blaze grew higher. The warmth felt good to both of them.

John sniffed the air inside the dome shelter. It smelled of woodsmoke and spruce, fresh-cut wood, a fragrance that seemed to ward off the cold of the ground, the dampness outside. The rain spattered on the branches above them, the sound a soothing patter that was almost hypnotic.

Ben dug out hardtack and some strips of jerky from his saddlebags and offered some to John. They chewed the modest fare, washing down the crumbs and small pieces of meat with water from their canteens.

"Might be we want to set watches, Johnny. One of us stay awake while the other sleeps. No tellin' about them jaspers. Might come sneakin' up on us, even in this rain."

"All right."

"I'll take the first one. Get yourself some sleep."

John was tired. So much had happened that day, he hadn't had time to think about fatigue. Now that he was warmed by the fire, his belly full, he felt his muscles relax and his eyelids grow heavy. He walked outside to relieve himself, then came back in and lay down on his bedroll.

"G'night, Ben," he said, closing his eyes.

"Sleep tight, Johnny."

The fire crackled, the rain seethed through the trees in a steady rhythm that lulled him to sleep within a few minutes. The scent of fresh-cut spruce was like a silent accompaniment to the lullaby of the rainfall.

The last thing he thought of was his father. He saw an image form in his mind, clear and vivid as if it were carved out of fine crystal. It seemed to him that he was there by the fire, smoking his pipe, listening to his wife read a poem from a book called

Leaves of Grass by a man named Walt Whitman. The poem was about the death of Abraham Lincoln, and he could hear his mother's dulcet voice intoning the words, as little Alice lay curled up on the floor at her feet, sound asleep. *"When lilacs last in the dooryard bloom'd . . ."*

12

As soon as Pete Rutter was out of earshot of the two men he had seen with Luke, he put the lash to his horse and rode at break-neck speed along the trail Ollie had followed bringing them all up there, and had taken going back to Fountain Creek. The rippling boom of thunder seemed to intensify his urgency to get away before those two came after him.

It was that pistol, he thought, and the man holding it. A young man, no more than a pup, but something about him, about the way he treated poor old Luke, sent shivers up Pete's spine and made him want to pee his pants. That face and those eyes. Didn't fit right on a man so young, he thought. Cold, hard black eyes. A face like a choir boy, but chiseled out of granite, the jawline hard as iron, and the way he had looked at Luke. That silver-filigreed Colt in his hand, so fine looking, so deadly, like a pretty snake a-settin' in the sunlight, its colors all shiny as satin and bright as a painted jewel box.

And that old bastard with the Yellow Boy. Pete had a furrow in his left shoulder where a .44/40 bullet had burned a crease like he'd been touched with a hot branding iron. And the left side of Pete's face was scratched up as if wild cats had been turned loose on him. The bastard had barked him with that big Henry, shot a bullet into the bark of a pine tree and sent splinters and a chunk square to the side of his head. He had a knot on his cheekbone big as a plum and probably just as purple. It hurt like fire, and that raw wound in his arm was burning with a fever all its own.

Pete was mad and scared, and he whipped his horse over the rocky, treacherous ground, speeding past trees and brush that just blurred in the corners of his eyes. Lightning burst through the black clouds like jagged rivers of mercury, frying the air itself and sending huge thunderboomers through the Sangre de Cristos like a battery of howitzers. Pete was sweating and feverish, but he was putting ground between himself and that old man and that strange boy with a Colt that had to be worth a good thousand dollars if it was worth a penny.

Rutter knew rain was going to catch him.

The very air felt heavy and wet to him and every splash of lightning made his skin jump, made him brace himself for the resulting crack of thunder that put spurs to his horse without his having to touch a spur to its tender flank.

Ollie and the others had not tried to conceal their tracks, and they left marks a blind man could follow. The earth was churned up where the ground was hard, intaglioed with hooved impressions where it was soft. The tracks grew fresher, so he knew he was getting close. He would not take the time to stop and squirrel into his slicker. The fear in him was too great. And he kept looking over his shoulder as if expecting the old man and the young man with the engraved Colt to come pounding down on him, their guns blazing, sounding like the bluster of thunder that cannoned over his head.

The air he breathed now had the taint of ozone. The hairs stood up on the back of his neck and arms. He dashed across a rocky flat and into more trees, then down a shallow bank where Ollie and the others had passed. Rutter rode into a clearing that widened into a meadow fringed by evergreens, and the roaring thunder dogged him as he drove his horse on, into a valley ringed by black clouds pushing against each other, setting off electrical charges that turned the darkness into day as lightning crackled in jagged latticework across a wide expanse. Smoke rose from an unseen tree that had been struck, high up on a slope of staggered pines, their tops shrouded in ground-hugging clouds.

Rutter rode right into a thin line of trees that petered out onto a shale-and-rock-strewn flat. A half dozen rifles bristled in a semicircle of men on bended knees, ready to blow him out of the saddle.

Rutter put on the brakes, jerking his reins back hard against his chest. His horse bent its head as the bit dug into its tongue and the corners of its mouth. The horse's rump dipped as its hind hooves dug in and skidded on plates of gray shale.

"Pete, you almost got your damned head blowed off," Ollie yelled as Rutter's body swayed backward, then forward as the horse came to a halt. Rutter had to grip the saddle horn to keep from being thrown out of the saddle.

Rutter gasped for breath as all of the men stood up and brought their rifles down from their shoulders. They were all wearing black slickers. They looked like a gathering of highwaymen, with their gleaming rifles and coats pulled back to reveal sidearms jutting from their holsters.

"Shit, you liked to scared me to death," Rutter said, his words rushing from his mouth in a breathy staccato.

"Better put on your soogan, Pete," Ollie said. "It's going to get mighty wet here pretty quick."

"Where's Luke?" Army growled.

"Fritz, bring the horses up," Ollie said. Then he turned back to Pete. "Yeah, where's Luke?"

"I-I reckon he-he's dead," Pete said, still panting from lack of breath. He hadn't realized how hard he had been riding and now that the juices of fear were subsiding in him, he was tired, his nerves jangling like a sackful of cowbells.

"What the hell?" Ollie said.

Fritz led the horses out from the trees. The other men took their reins from him and mounted.

"Ollie, let's get to that 'dobe camp," Mort said. "Else we're going to get fried by lightning or drowned by the damned rain."

"Yeah, yeah," Ollie said, taking the reins of his horse from Fritz. "You got some explaining to do, Pete."

Pete knew about the old adobe. They had spent the night there on the ride up to the mining camp. It was an old line shack used by sheepherders, long since abandoned, gone to cobwebs, spiders, rats, and mice, littered with the bones of small animals and human fecal matter. It wasn't a palace, but it had a thick sod roof and board shutters. It would keep most of the rain off their backs and be a lot warmer inside than out, once the storm hit.

The adobe cabin sat atop a hillock overlooking a broad shelf that formed part of a valley. There was a decrepit corral and a lean-to where the sheepherders had stored salt and mineral licks and other materials, such as medicines and stock tanks, wagons, and tools. The riders put their horses under the lean-to, tied them up, then stomped inside the filthy adobe while lightning played its light and energy on and inside the swollen black clouds that pressed down over the land. Thunder met thunder in a clash of sound as the storm began to converge and gather strength, the distant clouds already bursting their swollen bellies, dropping rain in dark, gauzy sheets that looked like veils of black ash.

A few minutes after the men entered the 'dobe, carrying their rifles and bedrolls, the wind blew the first smatterings of rain against the outer walls and shot spray inside. The building shook against the onslaught of a powerful gust, and they could almost feel the tug of the wind as it tried to rip off the sod roof.

"Whoo," Red Dillard exclaimed, "she's a blue norther."

Mort Anders leaned his rifle in a corner, kicking away little peppercorns of rat shit from under the place where he rested the stock.

"She's a blow," he said.

The wind licked at the shutters, rattling them as it sucked and pressed against the weathered wood. Then the rain struck the land around the shack, blasted against the mud-brick walls with tremendous force. The sound was like birdshot spattering against the walls and shutters. The wind howled like some wounded beast under the eaves, and the horses neighed in terror from under the lean-to.

As the men settled down and found places to sit or lean, Ollie dropped his gear and walked over to Rutter, his menacing bulk nearly dwarfing the man.

"I want to hear about them two men we missed up at that miner's camp, Pete. You put their lamps out? And what the hell happened to Luke?"

"Luke bought the farm, I reckon, Ollie.

And them two miners come down on us like a cartload of shit."

"What do you mean?"

"I mean they was comin' after all of us when me and Luke heard 'em. They had their rifles unlimbered and was followin' our tracks."

"You get a good look at them? And how come you didn't get the drop on 'em and rub 'em out?"

"Me and Luke split up so's we could dust them off when they rode past. Like, you know, we was flankin' 'em. I drew the old geezer, and he had him a Henry forty-four. Looky here what he done to me."

Pete slipped his slicker from his shoulder and showed everyone the torn shirt, the raw, bloody furrow in the meaty part of his upper arm. "And he barked me with his second shot, liked to took my head clean off."

He slipped the slicker back on the exposed shoulder and stuck his neck out so that Ollie and the others could see the side of his face that was scratched and scored by exploding pine bark.

"And then you shot that old geezer dead, right, Pete?"

"No, siree, that geezer had my number, sure as shit, and I lit a shuck. I heard some shots over to where Luke had gone and so I circled around with the field glasses to take a look. I figured I could maybe get a shot at the old fart 'cause he headed that way."

"And then what?" Ollie's query was accusatory, his tone laden with anger and impatience.

"The other jasper was a kid, not even twenty years old, I figured, and he had Luke down, blood all over him like he just butchered a hog."

"He shot Luke?"

"He gutted him like a fish. Luke was leaking bowels and beggin' the boy to put him out of his misery."

"Jesus," Army said.

By then, all the men had crowded around Pete to hear his story. They had him ringed and walled in. Pete was beginning to leak sweat like a skin sieve. His face was bathed in perspiration, droplets dripping from his brows, his nose, and his chin.

"What did the boy do?" Dick Tanner asked. He had a quirly in his mouth and struck a match to light it. The flare of the flame lit his eyes for a moment. They appeared, under Dick's thick brows, to bore straight into Pete's with diabolic intensity.

Pete blinked. He swallowed.

"I, ah, and this might sound funny," Pete

said, "but I think that pup was torturin' Luke. I couldn't hear what he said, but I bet he was askin' about all of us. And he had that Colt in his hand the whole time. A gun like I never seen before."

"You better explain that, Pete," Ollie said.

"Like I said, it was filigreed with silver. And I think them grips was ivory. Not pearl, but pure ivory. And that silver sparkled to beat hell."

"But you don't know what the kid did to Luke because you hightailed it out of there. Right, Pete?"

"Yeah," Pete said. "I got the hell out. You would have, too, Ollie. Luke wasn't goin' to make it, and it was two against one. I'd already got burnt twice and I didn't want to end up like Luke with my guts pourin' out of my belly."

Ollie said nothing. His jaw hardened and his face tightened into a mask that made Pete shrink back. The smoke from Tanner's cigarette hung in the air like a pall over Pete's head.

"It's just two of 'em," Army said, breaking the silence. "They come after us, they're worm meat."

Ollie fixed Army with a glare, his eyes burning through narrow slits like the eyes of a snake about to strike.

"Well, that kid is going to come after us, for sure," Ollie said. "You got to watch somebody like that."

"What do you mean?" Red Dillard asked.

"He's got something in his craw and he don't have no sense, Red. That makes him dangerous. He put Luke down and Luke probably spilled everything he knows about us."

"Hell, he's just a kid," Mort said. "Ain't he, Pete?"

"He's a kid what makes your skin crawl. You see him with that fancy pistol and you damned sure know he means business."

"Shut up, Pete. You had the chance to kill both the kid and the old man. 'Stead, you tucked your tail between your legs and run off like a scared possum."

"That ain't fair, Ollie. I was outnumbered."

"I ain't afraid of no kid," Army gruffed, swelling up his chest.

"Me, neither," Mort said.

Ollie threw a hand at all of them and turned away, lost in thought.

The windblown rain blasted the adobe, howled outside, and shot freshets of air through the shutters. A fine mist mingled with the smoke from Dick's cigarette and the room darkened until all the men were faceless shadows. There was only the orange glow from the tip of Dick's cigarette and a silence filling up with men's private thoughts.

Ollie stood there, as if listening to something besides the wind and the rain, something underneath, like hoofbeats or the tread of a man's boot. Silly, he thought. Nobody could ride down on them in such a violent storm.

Nobody, except a crazy kid with a fancy gun, and an old galoot packin' a Yellow Boy.

He felt itchy and his nerves put a tic on one side of his face. That was annoying because he couldn't stop it. That tic always hit him when he ran into something he didn't understand, or, like when he was a young boy listening to another kid tell a ghost story that made the hackles stiffen and shiver on the back of his neck.

It was that kind of a feeling, in that dark room, with shadowy men all around him all thinking the same thing.

That kid was going to hunt them down, and if he was crazy, maybe from grief, he was going to be dangerous.

There was fear in that room, Ollie thought. And some of it was infecting him, damn it all. It was fear of the unknown. The kind of fear that could take root in a man and turn his guts into a hatching of winged insects, all swarming and fluttering until a man's knees turned to jelly as he waited for a door to open, or someone to step out of nowhere with a gun his hand. Someone with the face of a kid and the heart of a killer bent on revenge.

Ollie took a breath and let it out as if it might relieve that nameless fear that was beginning to claw at him, to sniff inside his brain like some prowling beast that only hunted at night, in the darkness of a man's head.

13

The smoke rose to the top of the spruce-bough shelter, seeped through the limbs and needles. Ben fought through them with his hands, pushing the boughs, widening them to make a smoke hole. The burning pine made a lot of smoke, too much for the small enclosure. He widened the smoke hole and more smoke rose and flowed through into the night where the wind snatched it away, tore it to scraps of wispy confetti. Then, even these dissipated and vanished, becoming just so much atmosphere.

He looked down at John, who had not stirred. He looked so young when he was asleep, but young Savage had grown old in the space of a day. Shadows danced across John's face, chased by firelight the color of peaches. Firelight that painted the young man's face with its soft brush, flickered next to the hairline, shaped and reshaped John's nose and his chin, blurring the cheekbones in pastel light, bending the jawline up and down in the mystical play of those fluid shadows.

Some of the tiny pale hairs on John's face were beginning to curl like the curlicue appendages on baby pigs. In another few days, Ben thought, John would have to shave once again, and when he bent down for a closer look, he saw that there were little dark specks where the darker hairs were pushing up and Ben knew he'd be peppered with those in no time. The boy was growing into a man before his very eyes.

And he sat there, listening to the soothing sound of the rain, trying not to fall asleep. He put another small piece of rotting wood on the fire, inching it from the bottom with a gentle shove. Sparks rose inside the smoke, winking like tiny fireflies on a brief and dazzling flight. The smell of the wood smoke was almost as satisfying as that from a pipe with apple-scented tobacco and the loamy aromas of an Alabama field.

John slept deep beneath an ocean of soft rain and whispering wind through spruce boughs. He floated through October hills when the sumacs and the maples blazed with a vermilion fire and the oak leaves yellowed and browned in shady hollows and on the ridges where the white-tailed deer nibbled the last of the acorns while gray squirrels chattered on the slopes, their bottle-brush tails flicking nervously as they scurried through the skeletons of fallen leaves like fugitive church mice.

In the dream, John picked up dead leaves of various hues and stuffed them into an empty flour sack. The leaves kept changing shapes and textures. The maple and the sumac leaves were bleeding when he picked them up, and the yellow leaves ran like melted butter as he put them into the bag. The brown leaves sprouted little spindly legs and kicked the sides of the sack once they were inside.

He walked to a flat stone beneath a tall oak tree halfway up a deep hollow. He poured out the contents of the bag and then began stuffing them back in, squeezing the bag at various points to fashion legs and arms, feet and hands. The leaves changed into cloth scraps as he picked them up, and their colors bled through the sack as it took the shape of a rag doll. He made a face by squeezing the neck, and he picked up dead pine needles and used them for hair as they turned to brown yarn. He fixed acorns on the face for eyes and stripped a pinecone for teeth. He placed a hickory nut on the center for a nose.

He positioned the doll in the center of the flat rock, which transformed itself into a small bed with white sheets. He smoothed the air and it turned golden in the sunlight. The nose shaped itself and the brown teeth turned white and a small smiling mouth appeared, changed into a dazzling smile.

The rag doll spoke in a hollow, sepulchral voice.

"Mommy, Mommy," it cried and reached out to him. Its hand passed through his chest and clutched his heart. The little fingers squeezed his heart and the doll continued calling, "Mommy, Mommy."

Just before John awoke, the doll transformed itself again and became alive in the spitting image of his sister Alice. And this time, as its arms reached for him, it called out: "Johnny, Johnny."

"Hey, boy, you having a nightmare." Ben's voice boomed inside the shelter.

John opened his eyes and put up a hand to shield them from the firelight.

"Alice," John said. "I had a dream about Alice."

"You didn't sleep long. Hour and a half, two hours maybe. You want to go back to sleep?"

John shook his head.

"No. I couldn't. Not now."

"Wind's died down some. Not raining so hard."

"You better get some sleep, Ben. I'll tend the fire and keep a lookout."

"I could use a few winks."

John was wide awake when Ben curled up on his bedroll and closed his eyes. The dream had been disturbing, but he recognized it for what it was, a deep wish that he could bring Alice back to life, could once again hear her voice and her laughter. Now, in the darkness of night, the tragedy of her death became even more poignant and devastating to him. An innocent life snuffed out like a candle before she even had a chance to grow and learn and become.

He pushed down his anger, but he felt it boiling beneath the surface. He saw once again the faces of those responsible for the murders and his resolve quickened as he fed the fire and listened to the steady drone of falling rain. He watched the smoke rise through the widened hole in the spruce boughs, then looked at Ben, who had begun to snore softly. He was glad that Ben was still alive and with him. But he would have given anything to have had a rifle or pistol with him up in the mine. Now, he knew, he would never be caught like that again. He would always wear his pistol when awake, and he would track down those murderers if it took him the rest of his life.

Ben slept for better than four hours. John watched him awaken by himself and wondered why he wasn't sleepy. Then, a moment later, he knew why. The rain had stopped, and it meant that they could get on the trail of the outlaws again. He took some comfort in believing that they would have holed up during the night as well. He had no idea how far ahead of them Ollie and the others were, but he hoped, before day's end, he would pick up their tracks as they headed for Fountain Creek and Pueblo.

"You ain't sleepy, Johnny?"

John thought about it for a moment.

"Naw." He felt strangely alive, with even an electric tingle in his veins. In the cold of a pale dawn, with the sky like dirty cream, the tattered remnants of clouds floating in the sky like thin loaves of cotton, all desire for sleep had vanished. After such a dark night, the sun was a welcome harbinger of a day good for tracking. A day when murderous men might be caught up to and cornered, to meet justice at the business end of a Colt .45.

"I feel like I been dry washed in a big old milk churn and hung out on a damned clothesline. My eyes burn like they been rubbed with chili peppers, and there's places on my back I swear still got little sharp stones buried in 'em."

"That's just your age, Ben."

"Haw. Age ain't got nothin' to do with it. I got tender skin and I need eight good hours in the kip."

John laughed. "Let's get out of here," he said as he tied his bedroll behind his saddle. Ten minutes later they were back on the trail.

The land was drying up and there were piñons now among the pines, their seeds littering the ground like peppercorns. The sun was well up in the sky, still feeble as it fought through fleets of long, basking clouds. The back range was a faint blue ridge, and another behind that one was all gray and hazy, so far away a man could not reach it in a week.

"I feel like a new man, Ben. It's age, and you know it."

"Yair, your age gives your ball its bounce, Johnny. You don't need to lord it over me."

"Sleep in the saddle, then, Ben. I'm the one watching for tracks."

"The onliest tracks you're gonna see this mornin' is made by runnin' water. Them cutthroats probably rode all night, that gold burnin' holes in their pockets."

"No, I figure they holed up somewhere. I feel it in my bones, Ben. I can almost smell 'em."

And then they saw the 'dobe, one wall burnished a rich golden tan by the sun. John reined up, caught by surprise. Ben let out a long sigh.

"Well, well, well," Ben said. "What do we have here?"

"That's damned sure on the trail them fellers took. Tracks were washed away, but the trail now, that's been standing out clear."

"Johnny, all I can say is you're a born tracker. I thought we was just ridin' aimless."

"I'll bet Ollie and his bunch holed up there to ride out the storm."

"What gives you that idea?"

"A feeling."

"A feeling? That's all?"

"Ben, did you ever think you could read another man's thoughts? I mean . . ."

"I know what you mean. Nope. I ain't no clairvoyant."

"Neither am I, but sometimes I think you can get into a man's mind, like if he lets his thoughts loose to float out there where a man can pick them up. I think those men stayed in that adobe shack last night. I can smell fresh horseshit."

"Maybe they're still in there, all of 'em. Asleep."

John slipped the Winchester from its scabbard. He and Ben had both cleaned their rifles and pistols before setting out that morning. He looked at the surrounding terrain, checking specifically for high points overlooking the adobe. There were none within rifle range. The shack appeared to be atop a shelf overlooking a large plain. Anyone approaching from the other side, the front, could be seen for a long way.

"What're you gonna do, Johnny?"

"We're going to circle that 'dobe, Ben. You head off to the right and I'll take the left. We'll just see if there are any horses down there under that lean-to."

"And if there ain't?"

"We'll look for tracks. Go on. Keep an eye out."

The two rode off in opposite directions. They made a wide arc, keeping to the scattered scrub pines and piñons, riding slow so that the horses didn't dislodge any rocks that would clatter and give them away.

John stopped his horse less than a hundred yards from the lean-to. He stared at the adobe, looking for any signs of life. The lean-to appeared to be empty. There was no movement. The adobe sat there, seemingly deserted, silent as a monument of stone. He was looking for movement, the flick of a horse's tail, the head of a man, the barrel of a rifle.

Ben appeared on the other side. He stopped his horse, cupped a hand to one ear, and listened. He scanned the front of the adobe and the surrounding plain of grass. Then he raised a hand and waved to John. John waved back and coaxed his horse closer to the shack.

There, he found what he was looking for, in and around the lean-to, and in front of the adobe itself: fresh tracks of horses and men. His heart began to pound in his chest, throb in his temples. He looked down on the long plain and saw nothing. Ben rode up, and he, too, was looking at the ground.

"Looks like your hunch was right, Johnny. These are fairly fresh tracks."

"How fresh?"

Ben kneaded his forehead with his thumb and index finger.

"Two hours. Maybe more. Maybe a mite less."

"This is where they stayed, Ben."

The front door was ajar. John dismounted and signed for Ben to cover him. He stepped to the door and listened. Then he slipped inside. The smell of urine was strong, stinging the delicate membrane of his nostrils. As his eyes adjusted to the light, he saw depressions on the filthy floor where men had lain on blankets. There were a lot of boot tracks in the loose dirt.

"Anything there?" Ben called.

"They were here."

John stepped from the adobe, stood in the sunlight, breathing clean air.

"Stinks in there, eh?" Ben said.

"To high heaven."

"So, that bunch is a couple of hours ahead of us. Whilst you was inside, I been studying the tracks. They go in a straight line down into that plain, like they was headed due east."

"To Fountain Creek," John said, climbing back on Gent.

"Likely," Ben said.

"Let's follow 'em out." John tapped Gent's flanks with his spurs and turned him toward the maze of tracks leading off the shelf and down into the flat. They rode straight into the sun and lowered their heads to shade their eyes with their hat brims. An eagle floated down from the high country and traversed the space above the plain, touching the air currents with its wingtips to stay aloft. Its head moved from side to side as he searched for small game, anything alive that moved.

On the other side of the plain, they rode into scrub pines and brush. Beyond were low foothills in shadow, but there were enough trees to conceal them from anyone watching from atop the nearest ridge.

The tracks were plain, and then they all converged at an open spot. The tracks were a moil of hoofmarks in a small circle. John studied them for a long moment, then rode beyond and saw something that brought him up short. He turned to Ben.

"Looks like they did some talking here," he said. "And now look. They split up."

Ben rode up and saw what John was seeing. Four sets of tracks continued on to the east. Three other sets broke off and headed north.

"What do you make of it, Ben?"

"You're asking me? You're the one with the hunches, Johnny."

A light breeze rivered through the trees, brushed their faces. It carried the smells of pine and new earth freshly washed by the rain. They heard the shrill scream of the eagle and when they looked to the sky, the eagle was nowhere in sight.

"Well, they could be splitting up so they can ambush us," John said. "Or those three riding off to the north might be heading for the Springs or Denver. Maybe to meet up later."

"Which ones do we follow?"

John rode around, leaning over to bring the ground closer to his eyes. He reined up and pointed east.

"I know the horse Ollie is riding. Its hooves sink deeper than the others because he's the biggest man. He's heading for Fountain Creek and likely following it right into Pueblo. I don't know about those other three. We'll just have to keep an eye out."

"We been doin' that."

"Yeah, but I think we've seen the last of those three for a while."

A few yards farther on, the tracks showed that Ollie and those with him had put spurs to their horses and were running them at a gallop. The sight of the churned-up earth quickened John's pulse. But he was not about to chase them at the same speed.

Ollie and the others might be counting on his trackers doing just that.

And he and his cronies might be waiting just ahead, hiding somewhere, ready to shoot him and Ben out of their saddles.

"They're on the run, Johnny."

"I know. But we're going to take it slow, Ben. Pueblo's not going anywhere. And we know where to find Ollie. I'm betting he doesn't know that."

"Seems to me you're betting on a whole lot without ever seeing this Ollie's hand."

"I'm reading his mind," John said, and his mouth bent in a wry smile.

The mountains behind them lit up as the sun rose and the distant snowcaps gleamed like ancient beacons, as billions of tiny ice crystals reflected the sunlight from countless prisms.

And the eagle returned to the sky and floated down the long river of wind, skimming the treetops, heading, perhaps, for Fountain Creek, just as they were. His snowy head glistened like the far-off peaks that outlined the top of the world in dazzling splendor as if created solely to capture the sun's light in their snowy keeps.

14

Rutter was angry at Ollie's decision to split up the bunch. Tanner and Anders sided with Pete because Ollie had picked them to go with Rutter.

"Well, I want a split of that dust right here and now," Rutter said, his Germanic accent fighting with the drawl of the Mississippian. That was always the way it was when Pete's ire was up. The v's kept crowding out the w's, and vice versa.

"I'll give you boys some of the dust, but not until we meet up in Rosa's Cantina."

"I want mine now," Rutter said.

"You didn't finish the job I sent you and Luke to do, Pete. Now, you got to pay for that mistake. We got two rifles on our ass and you're going to take them out before you share in the rewards. Got that?"

"I don't like it none," Pete said.

"Tough shit." Ollie looked ready to drive a hammy fist through Pete's beard.

"So, you want us to cover your backtrail and rub them two miners out before we get any of the gold?"

"That's as plain as I can put it, Pete. And every second you spend here arguing about it gets them two just that much closer to us."

"Hell," Tanner said, "it's seven against two? Why don't we just wait it out and bushwhack 'em when they come ridin' down on us?"

"Because that's just what they might expect, Dick."

"So? We still outnumber them," Anders said.

"And so do the three of you, Mort. Look, I thought about this. I'm sending Pete with you boys because he's the only one who knows what those two miners look like. None of us has seen their faces. And I figure you and Dick are about the best shots in the bunch. I expect you'll make short work of those two pilgrims and won't be more than two or three hours behind us getting to Pueblo."

"It's that kid," Pete said. "Something about him."

"What about him?" Ollie asked.

"I don't know, Ollie. He just struck me as bein' different. The way he looked at Luke.

I mean he didn't have no pity or nothin'. And he brought Luke down. Hell, that surprised me more than anything."

"What do you mean, Pete?" Dick asked.

"Yeah, I'd like to know, too," Mort said.

Pete looked back in the direction from where they had come that morning. The sky was blue as cobalt, peaceful. The far mountains had that soft purple cast to them and the high peaks rose up above them, their snowy mantles so white a man couldn't look at them without going blind.

"Luke was the smartest man I ever knew. He was quick with a gun, wise as a fox. I mean, you never got the drop on old Luke. He was plenty savvy and he never blinked when it come to killin' a man. All the time I seen him lyin' there, his guts spillin' out of him like snakes, I kept wonderin' how in hell that kid took him down. And Luke looked downright pitiful, like that shiny blue-black Colt all scrolled with silver scared the hell out of him. And I never knew Luke to be afraid of nothin'."

"That pistol the kid had," Ollie said. "It's really got you spooked, eh, Pete?"

Rutter looked at Ollie and bristled.

"It wasn't just the damned pistol. It was something about that kid. Maybe the look in his eyes. He must have belonged to that woman we kilt, and maybe his daddy was one of 'em we rubbed out. And that little gal."

"You shut up about that kid," Ollie said. "Some things is best forgot."

"Well, that young feller had something in his craw that wasn't natural, Ollie. And where does a kid like him get a gun like that? And he beat Luke, damn it. He beat him like Luke was nothin'. Watched him die real slow and enjoyed hisself."

"You think he's, ah, experienced? I mean, he's an owlhooter like us?"

"I don't know. He just had that look about him. Make the hairs stiffen up on the back of your neck. That kind of look."

"Well, then you'd better shine bright, Pete," Ollie said. "Shoot him dead before you start havin' nightmares about him."

"I already got 'em," Pete said.

"I ain't afraid of no snot-nose kid," Dick said.

"Me, neither," Mort said, drawing himself up as if ready to do battle.

Ollie nodded at the three of them.

"I wish we could all go after him," Pete said, a wistful whine to his voice.

Hobart had reached the limit of his patience. He snorted at Pete and his face hardened into a mask that reflected the anger rising to the surface. He narrowed his eyes and the look bore right into Pete's.

"Pete, you get your thumb out of your butt and ride out. We'll see you in Pueblo."

Rutter opened his mouth to say something, but clamped it shut against the brute force of Ollie's withering glare. The three men turned their horses and rode away, taking a northwesterly tack.

They didn't see the smile on Ollie's face, but the others who were there with him did.

"You don't want them to come back, do you, Ollie?" Red said.

"I don't give a damn. More gold for the rest of us if they don't."

Fritz finished swallowing water from his canteen, wiped his mouth with his sleeve.

"Could be you don't want to split with nobody, Ollie."

"Fritz, you got a mouth on you. Better button it up 'fore I shut it for good."

"You're pretty testy this morning, Ollie," Dillard said.

"Something stuck in your craw, too, Red?" Ollie glared at him.

"It's just that you have all the gold, Ollie. We don't have shit. And it's beginning to look like you might want it all for yourself. If you don't expect Mort, Pete, and Dick to come back . . ."

"I expect them to kill those two jacka-napes on our trail, Red. And then meet us at Rosa's. It don't need to be complicated. Now, if you gents are ready, let's ride to the Fountain and water our horses. Fact is, I sent them three to do the job because they're better'n any of you when it comes to killin' snakes."

They all shut up then, but Ollie knew their thoughts were running faster than their mouths. It was the gold, he knew. It made men crazy even when it was in the ground or at the bottom of a creek. But now, knowing that he had it all in his saddlebags was beginning to eat at them. He didn't trust a one of them. And, he knew, none of them trusted him.

He had chosen this route carefully, avoiding the larger towns like Colorado Springs and Canon City. By taking a direct route to Fountain Creek, they kept away from settlements and people. He knew that packing that much gold would cause tongues to wag no matter where they wound up and converted the dust to cash. But Pueblo was a better place than Denver, he reasoned, even though he liked Denver better than Pueblo. Pueblo was a more tolerant place, a kind of crossroads between Denver, Taos, and Santa Fe, with many people coming and going.

Strangers did not cause as much stir in Pueblo as they did in Denver or the smaller Colorado Springs. In Pueblo, they would hardly be noticed. And it was probably easier to change dust into greenbacks, with fewer questions asked. But there was another reason Hobart was anxious to get to Pueblo, to Rosa's Cantina. Rosa Delgado was that reason.

"You still got them field glasses, Pete?" Tanner asked, as they were moving up to a higher elevation and starting their swing back toward the trail they had taken down from Cripple Creek.

"Yeah, I got 'em."

"See that little hill yonder?" Dick pointed.

"I see it."

"I noticed that when we rode down. It's right near the trail. We could go up there and watch for them two pilgrims, pick 'em off real easy."

"Good idea," Anders said.

"Safer than huntin' them higher up where the trees is thicker," Dick said.

Pete was relieved. He was glad Dick and Mort were with him. The three of them ought to be able to handle that old galoot and the boy.

A flock of doves flew out of the piñons as

they rode through them. Their wings whistled like tiny flutes as they passed, twisting in the air like gray corkscrews, and then they were dark, silent specks in the sky until they vanished in the scrub along the lower slopes. A quail piped from somewhere in the distance, a plaintive call that made the back of Pete's neck prickle as if spiders with hairy feet and fuzzy legs were crawling up to his hairline.

The call reminded him of when he and Luke were waiting for those two survivors of the mining camp. They had tried to imitate the quail's whistle, using it as a signal to each other that they were there, waiting and ready. Their whistles must not have fooled the old man and the boy.

They reached the little knoll and when they got there, Pete pulled the field glasses from his saddlebags and slung them around his neck. There were a few scrub pines for cover, their dwarfed trunks bent by wind and weather, stunted. Little water held to the ground in such a place. But they had a good view of a long stretch of trail. It was a good enough place for an ambush.

"If we get off our horses," Mort said, "we'd have some cover. Not much, but some."

"Good idea," Dick said, swinging out of

the saddle. He jerked his rifle from its sheath once he was on the ground. It was a Winchester '73, loaded with .44/40 cartridges. He levered one into the chamber and stood behind one of the scrub pines.

Mort and Pete dismounted, too, and took their rifles in hand, moving to cover, their boots scraping on rocks. A clump of prickly pear clung to the hillside, its spines running with sunlight as if they were liquid. Pete stepped around it and knelt down behind one of the small trees. He leaned his rifle toward it, nestled the barrel on a crotch where he could reach it easily and quickly.

He put the glasses to his eyes and focused on the highest point of the trail. The glasses filled with trees and rocks and he swept them wide and then up and down.

"See anything?" Mort asked.

"Yeah, I see something."

"Them?"

"No, just trees. The trail. You think they're just going to ride up now that we're here waiting for them?"

"No need to get smart about it, Pete."

"Well, if I'd a seen 'em, I'd have called it out, Mort."

Mort didn't respond. He knelt down, too, and smoothed a place for his left knee. That didn't help. Small stones dug into his flesh.

Ants scurried from a small mound nearby. Mort looked at their red-and-black bodies, their quivering antennae, their spindly nervous legs. He began to sweat as the sun bore down on them.

"I hate waiting," Dick said, after a while. "And we got ants up here. Long as we don't bother 'em, maybe they'll leave us alone."

"Shut up, Dick," Mort said. "Sound carries a long way up here."

Dick nodded.

They waited, listening.

Pete glassed the trail, steadied on the trees that hid what was above them. His knee hurt from his weight pressing it down into the sharp pebbles. An ant crawled across the toe of his boot. He stood up.

"Whatcha doin', Pete?" Dick asked.

"Leg's goin' numb."

"Yeah." Dick stood up, too, flexed the leg he had been leaning on to bring back the circulation. Mort looked at them and licked dry lips. He lifted his knee slightly and rubbed it.

"Yeah," Mort said. "Time for a stretch. Hell, them two might take hours to get down this far."

Then, they all stiffened as they heard a clatter of rocks up in the trees where the trail emerged.

"What was that?" Pete said, clawing for the field glasses.

"Take a look," Dick said, holding his rifle in front of his chest with both hands, ready to bring it to his shoulder.

Mort assumed a fighting stance as Mort *Pete* brought the glasses up and pressed them against his eyes.

A horse emerged from the line of trees, trailing its reins.

"What the hell . . ." Pete said.

"Ain't nobody on that horse," Mort said, in a gravelly whisper.

"Shh," Dick said.

The horse braced itself as it slowly stepped down the trail's incline.

Pete took the glasses away from his eyes, reached down, and grabbed his rifle.

The horse stopped, whickered. Then it turned its head and looked back up into the trees.

Pete's mouth went dry.

Ollie and his men negotiated a dry wash. The horses' hooves rang on stone as they stepped across the rocky flat.

They all reined up a second later when they heard, far off in the distance, the faint crack of a rifle. The sound echoed down to the them, sounding like the sharp snap of a bullwhip.

Then the sound died away into a deep silence. The horses stood like statues, leg muscles quivering, chests flexing with the rhythm of their breathing.

It was a long time, or seemed so, before they heard another rifle report. This one made a different sound, deeper, louder, not as sharp-edged, and the echoes seemed to go on forever as it sought that same desolate silence as before.

Ollie felt his throat go dry and begin to crack inside as if suddenly parched for no good reason.

An odd feeling came over him. He didn't like it because he couldn't define it. It felt as if some voice inside him was telling him to run, to ride fast and never look back.

It wasn't fear, exactly, but it was a crawling thing inside his mind, a creature that bore no name and made no sense.

The feeling he had just then was that he had heard rifles firing, but they were so far away that he could not put faces to the shooters. It seemed, he thought, as if those rifles had been fired by ghosts.

And who was dead? Who was going to die?

His hands turned clammy with sweat, and his skin crawled with centipedes as if someone had walked across his grave.

15

The morning sun stirred up breezes on the Great Plains. Its heat warmed the land, generating vagrant currents of air that swirled and mixed with the cool zephyrs surging lazily down from the Rocky Mountains. Small whirlwinds, dust devils, churned across the grasslands, whipping up dirt and pollen in their vortices, dancing across gullies and washes like some capricious dervishes, before gusting into life-less dust that floated back to earth and vanished. As the sun's rays burned ever westward, warming the cold earth, molding the wet clay and the mud, the breezes soared and sank, blended with other air currents high and low, whispering through brush and trees, carrying scraps of messages in its currents and sounds it gathered along the way, dashing some to pieces, lifting others on invisible pinions that carried them far before dropping them like dust from the brief flights of ephemeral whirlwinds.

The breeze blew against John's face and he heard small bits of garbled sound that made no sense at first. Then, his senses interpreted those sounds as fragments of human speech, far off voices that faded in and out, as if a passing wind had listened in to a conversation and carried pieces of voices and words that made no sense, but were clearly identifiable.

He stopped his horse and held up a hand. Ben halted his horse, too.

"Listen," John said.

But the scrambled voices died away and the zephyrs carried only the whispers of a light breeze.

Then John heard it again. A man's voice. Then another, different voice on top of that one. It was almost maddening because he could not pinpoint the speakers nor the direction from which the sounds had come. Yet, they came from the east, below him. He wet a finger and held it up. Yes, the light breeze was coming from the east, from the lower elevations below them. Not on the trail, but from another place, off to the left.

"You hear it, Ben?"

Ben shook his head.

John pointed off to the left, cupped his

ear to pick up the sounds.

A rattle of rocks so far away his ear might have been fooled. Then, a low voice, a human voice, bearing part of a word, pieces of a sentence full of gaps and holes.

He turned back to look at Ben.

Ben shrugged. John pointed to his own ear, then nodded in the direction from which the sounds had come.

Ben cupped his ear and leaned forward in the saddle.

"Da . . . Ol . . . Pue . . . Foun . . . qua . . . ick . . ."

"I hear 'em," Ben said, in a loud whisper. "Far away. Down in there somewhere. Men on horseback, maybe. Comin' this way."

"Let's see who it is," John said, easing his rifle from its scabbard. Ben pulled the Henry up by the stock and rested it on the shoulder of his pommel.

The two rode down to the fringe of trees and dismounted. John slipped his rifle from its scabbard. On foot, they walked to the trees that halted at the rimrock of the shelf they were on and peered down at the open valley dotted with scrub and rocks, clumps of chaparral and cactus. There, on the knoll, they saw the three men crouched down, rifle barrels glinting in the sun.

"Yonder's the one that got away from you,

187

Ben," John whispered. "The one called Pete."

"I recognize him. Them other two look familiar."

"One is called Dick, and I think the other one is named Mort."

"You got a good memory."

John said nothing. He studied the men. They were within rifle range, but their bodies were concealed. A bullet could deflect and they could turn their rifles toward them and return fire.

He gestured to Ben as he stepped back from the tree cover. Ben followed him until they were back where they had ground-tied their horses.

"We got to get their attention," John said. "I want 'em standing up."

"How you figure to do that?"

"Give me a minute."

Several seconds went by and John heaved a sigh.

"They're watching the trail," he said. "Lookin' for us."

"I reckon."

"If you were to run Gent down there, they'd see my horse and maybe come out of hiding."

"They might shoot your horse just for practice, Johnny."

"I want to make that Pete pay for what he done, Ben. If you were to ride up behind Gent, but keep to cover, you might get one of the others."

"I might. I might get one. What about you? You'll be afoot."

"I'll walk down there and take out the other one if I can."

"Might be best to shoot their horses first. Then they can't get away."

John's forehead wrinkled as he gave that idea some thought.

"I'm still going to dust that Pete."

"Sure."

"You shoot the claybank and that bay. The sorrel belongs to Pete. I'll put that one down if I can."

"Their rifles will be barking, too, you know."

"I know. Those men came back to pick us off, Ben. I think Ollie and the others are riding toward Fountain Creek."

"What makes you think that?"

"Those three don't look too happy. I think they were left behind to finish us off, while the others rode on to Pueblo."

"Reading minds again?"

"Nobody down there except those three. Beyond where they sit, there's no cover in range. I think these three are by their lonesome."

Ben snorted.

"Sounds logical."

John snickered at the two-bit word. But it was the right word.

"Let's do it. Don't drive Gent down the trail out in the open until I have time to get set."

"I won't be able to see you, Johnny."

"Give me five minutes. I'll be set by then."

"Done," Ben said. He mounted Dynamite. John handed him Gent's reins.

"Good hunting, Ben," John said.

"You, too, Johnny."

John walked back to where they had observed the three men on the knoll. He lost sight of Ben, but could hear the faint chink of iron hooves on stone. He walked to the edge of the tree line and saw that the three outlaws were still there, squatting behind scrub pines, watching the trail.

He had been counting, trying to measure the minutes. Now he pushed the numbers out of his mind and concentrated on Pete, who was nearest him. A flicker of doubt ticked a corner of his mind. It was one thing to shoot at a man in self-defense, another to just kill a man who had no idea a bullet was coming in his way.

Was what he was about to do right? He was going to kill a man in cold blood. Just shoot him. End his life forever.

He thought about Alice and his mother, his father. He thought about all the others those men had helped slaughter. None of those murdered had stood a chance against these heartless killers. They deserved to die, maybe in the same manner. The flicker of doubt quivered, wavered, then vanished as he thought about those three men, what they had done, the looks on their faces when they had shot dead all of his friends and family.

Then he saw Gent out of the corner of his eye. The horse stepped out, down the trail, its reins dragging in the dirt. The man named Pete stood up and then reached down for his rifle.

John brought the Winchester to his shoulder. He eased the hammer back to full cock, squeezing the trigger slightly, so that the mechanism made only a dull scraping sound. He set the blade front sight on Pete's face, square on the nose. He brought the rifle into alignment so that the blade dissected the rear sight slot. He drew in a shallow breath. His finger took up the slack in the trigger and he squeezed.

The rifle bucked against his shoulder with

the force of the recoil as the powder exploded. White smoke and sparks spewed from the muzzle and he thought he could hear the whiz of the bullet as it sped toward its target.

Pete's face caved in just above the bridge of his nose. Blood spurted from the hole. The back of his skull flew off like a fragment of pottery and John could see the rosy spray, like a mist, burst from his head. The rifle dropped from his hands and clattered on stone, rustled the branches of the tree next to him. Pete's legs folded up and he crumpled, falling backward as his body twisted awkwardly, all mental control gone. He sprawled there, his body twisted, a lifeless heap.

John heard the bark of the Henry, then saw the claybank stagger before its forelegs folded up and his head dipped. A flower of blood blossomed on the horse's chest, a single jet spurting out as the bullet smashed muscle, severed an artery. The horse went down with a crash and the other two outlaws swung their rifles, seeking targets.

John jumped down from the rimrock and ran toward the knoll. He jacked another shell into the firing chamber, then carried the rifle in his left hand.

Ben emerged from cover and rode down

Gent's path, his reins looped around the saddle horn, his rifle scanning back and forth with its snout until it barked again.

Mort saw John running toward him. He turned and swung his rifle in a short arc. He fired, and the bullet whined off a rock, several yards from John.

Dick turned and grabbed up the reins of Pete's horse just as his own horse went down, a bullet in its neck.

Mort shouted at Dick.

"Don't leave me," Anders said, as John closed the distance.

"Look out," Tanner yelled.

Mort spun around to look at John. Ben was riding toward them now, too, Dynamite at a lope.

Tanner seemed frozen where he stood, holding the reins of Pete's horse, his own horse lying on the ground, its legs jerking in the final spasms of death.

Both men stared at Savage as he drew his pistol, the pistol Pete had told them about. They saw the flash of its silver and the blue-black sheen of its bluing. They saw, too, the look on Savage's face.

"You're him," Mort said, and clawed for his own pistol as he let the Spencer repeater drop onto a tree branch.

John saw the look on Mort's face and then

that same face flashed through his mind, the same face he had seen on the man who shot down Lee at close range, a quirky smile of savagery on his lips. The pasty skin beneath his beard as he rode down on Lee and blew his face away with that same pistol now leaping into his hand.

Tanner stared at John, at that silver-inlaid Colt, and turned quickly, grabbing the saddle horn of Pete's horse and hauling himself onto the saddle. He spurred the horse just as Ben fired again. But the bullet sizzled harmlessly over Tanner's head as Dick wheeled the horse and charged down from the knoll. He rode away, using the hillock for cover, his heart in his throat as he waited for a pistol to fire. Either Mort's or the kid's. He wondered if he would be able to tell the difference.

Ben cursed as he saw Tanner ride away, the hillock blocking most of his view. He saw only a bobbing black hat and a horse's rump.

John went into a fighting crouch as he thumbed back the hammer of his Colt.

Mort's pistol barrel was just clearing leather when John fired. He was no more than fifteen yards from Anders. He felt the pistol jump as the .45 cartridge exploded. Felt the pressure against the heel of his palm. But he held tight and the pistol stayed level as fire belched from its throat.

The bullet smashed into Mort's abdomen, just below the ribcage. He buckled and bent over slightly from the impact, from the terrible burn of pain as the bullet coursed through his innards, ripping through his stomach and tearing a chunk of intestine to shreds before it lodged in a muscle near his spine, flattened lead like the jagged head of a mushroom.

"Ah." Mort sighed, and sank to his knees. His fingers went slack and his pistol hit the rocky ground with a dull thunk. He grabbed his stomach and bright, fresh blood painted his fingers and wrists.

John closed the gap between him and Mort. Smoke seeped from the barrel of his pistol as he thumbed back the hammer, spinning the cylinder onto a fresh centerfire round. He looked into Mort's eyes as the man sank down on his legs. His eyes burned a final brightness as tears welled up in them and spilled onto his cheeks.

Mort's eyes turned to glass.

He opened his mouth to say something, but the only sound that came out was a low groan.

Ben rode up, saw that Tanner had left the plain and was no longer in sight.

"He's done for, Johnny," Ben said quietly.

"He's got him a minute to think about why he's dying like this."

Mort's eyes flickered with a final light.

"Torture," he rasped. "You . . ."

John bent down, holding the barrel of his pistol to Mort's throat.

"Hell's waiting for you, Mort, and I'm in no hurry. Take all the time you want."

"Jesus," Ben said, and turned away. The look on John's face was almost rapturous, unnatural, an alarming sight to see.

Mort gurgled in his throat. His eyes fluttered for a moment as he gasped for one last breath.

It didn't come. A frost seeped over his eyes. They went dull as pewter as if a shadow had stolen the light. He voided himself as he sank down, every useless muscle relaxed in death. The stench rose to John's nostrils and he backed away, stood up straight.

"Can't you just kill 'em clean, Johnny?" Ben said, his voice just above a whisper.

"Go catch up Gent, Ben. Maybe we can catch that Dick feller who got away."

"Yeah, anything to get away from this place."

John looked at Mort's face one last time. He looked at his own hands. They were steady. He worked a bullet from his cartridge belt, put the pistol on half cock and turned the cylinder and opened the gate. He stopped where the cap was dented, worked the rod to eject the shell, then slid in the fresh cartridge. He looked once more at the bloody face of Pete, a feeling of revulsion rising up in him. Not revulsion at what he had done, but at what Pete and the others had done. Those despicable acts of murder. It wasn't enough that these two were dead. The worst of the murderous bunch were still alive. Their faces burned into his mind. He walked down off the mound, heading toward Ben, who had Gent's reins in his hand and was turning Dynamite around to head back to pick him up. He holstered his pistol and slung his rifle over his shoulder.

"Three down," he said. "Five to go."

And those five, the hardest, he knew. Dick would tell them what had happened here and they would be warned. They would be waiting for him and Ben. They would have to look at every stranger harder than before. They would jump at every squeak of a door opening. They would reach for their pistols at every shadow. They would sleep with one eye open.

As Ben approached, leading Gent, John

looked up at the blue sky, at the distant range of mountains. None of it seemed real to him at that moment. It was just too peaceful and he still had the smell of burnt powder in his nostrils. And, still there, the scent of blood and death.

And the faces of the killers, those now dead, and those still alive.

Those still waiting for him. Looking over their shoulders. Watching for what surely was to come.

Death. Justice.

16

John cupped his hands to his mouth, faced east where Dick Tanner had escaped, and shouted at the top of his lungs: "I'm John Savage, Dick. I'm John Savage, Dick. Tell Ollie I'm coming." His voice echoed off the rimrock and traveled in a half circle, bouncing off rocks and stone bluffs until it faded away in the distance.

"Reckon he heard you?" Ben said with dry sarcasm.

"I don't know. Maybe."

"If I was you, I wouldn't advertise where I was goin'."

"I want Ollie and the others to know I'm coming to kill them."

"That's a mighty bold ambition, Johnny. And maybe dumb, too. That Ollie will be on the lookout for you if that man Dick heard your name and got your message."

John slipped his Winchester back in its scabbard. He reloaded his pistol, spun the cylinder. He set the cylinder so that the hammer was in between two cartridges, set the hammer at half cock, and slipped the Colt back in his holster. He climbed up on Gent's back and looked Ben square in the eyes.

"Ben, any time you want to go back to camp and blow holes in the mountain, you just ride on back."

"You want me to go?"

"That's your call, Ben."

"No, I want to know what you want. If you think I'm in the way, or hinderin' you, just let me know. I can find my way back to my mine."

"I welcome your company, Ben. I don't welcome your criticism about what I do."

"Seems like when a man's got somethin' to hide, every word spoke to him is a mite like criticism, Johnny."

"I got nothin' to hide," John said quickly. Too quickly.

"Didn't say you did, son. But if I call you on some things, it's 'cause I mean you well. Ain't criticism. Just observation, maybe."

"You got any other observations, Ben?"

"Just this, John Savage. You're mighty fast with that six-gun. I thought that feller Mort had you beat. I've seen some fast draws in my time, but yours beats all."

"You're observing this, or criticizing it?"

"You don't watch it, Johnny, you're liable to get a reputation."

The two began to ride away from the knoll. They followed Tanner's tracks, then veered back to the original trail they had been following. Both men took out their rifles and rested them on the pommels of their saddles. They spoke in low tones so they could hear any alien sound.

"A reputation? What's that mean?"

"It means, if word gets around that you're faster on the draw than anybody else, every young gunslinger within earshot is going to come after you."

"Why?"

"Because that's how the hotheads get their reputations. And they want reputations, them young slicks. Oh, how they want reputations."

"That's stupid."

"Stupid or not, that's the way things is, Johnny. Heed my words."

Hunger gnawed at John's stomach. He reached back and felt through his saddlebag for something to chew on, hardtack, jerky, whatever his fingers could find. He found a strip of jerky, put it in his mouth. The juices started flowing.

"Want some, Ben?"

"Naw, my belly's a little squirrely after seeing that Pete's head blow apart from a .44/40 chunk of lead."

"He's the one you missed."

"I didn't miss him. I just didn't hit him real square the first time. Did you see his arm? His sleeve?"

"No. I was looking at what was left of his ugly face."

"I put a bullet burn on him, and the side of his face that wasn't ruint by your bullet had marks on it."

"Marks?"

"Ever bark a squirrel?"

"No, but I heard about men doing that down in Arkansas. They shoot right next to a squirrel's head, right at the bark. The bark hits 'em in the head and kills 'em without leaving a mark. So they say."

"Well, it's true. And that's what I done to that Pete feller. Barked him like a damned squirrel. Whoo, I bet that stung him some."

John chuckled.

"So, Pete was really living on borrowed time. If he hadn't run off up there, you'd have dropped him for sure."

"Hard to shoot a man in the back. If he was runnin' off, I might have let him go."

"You ain't serious, Ben."

"No? Maybe I am. I guess I ain't got the

stomach for such. A man comes at me with a loaded gun, that's something different."

"Even a man like Pete? You saw what he done up there to our friends and kin."

Ben sighed.

"I reckon I look at things different," he said. "I figger a man pays for what he does somewhere down the road. Ain't up to me to be judge, jury, and hangman."

A young bull elk bugled off in the distance, far up in the pines. It was so faint, John barely heard it, and for several seconds afterward, he wondered if he had heard it at all. Elk usually didn't come down this low in the summertime, and it was early for the young bulls to be calling. They weren't even in the velvet yet.

The tracks they were following were plain. The wet ground had let the hooves sink in deeper, and there were clumps of mud thrown off by their passing. But the ground was drying out fast, with the sun and the breeze, and they were in the foothills, the far ranges just pale blue outlines jagged against the sky, and the high peaks were losing their luster, the white peaks not shining so bright as they moved toward the plain.

They found the place where Dick joined the trail behind Ollie and the others. John pointed to the sign.

"That Dick feller's in a powerful hurry," Ben said. "He come in here at a gallop."

"And still galloping, from the looks of the tracks."

"Ollie and them others are just keepin' up a steady pace, looks like."

"We'll see how fast they run when Dick catches up to them."

An hour later, John and Ben were descending onto another flat, a small valley ringed by low hills. The scents were different here, a hint of cactus flowers and sage woven in the breeze, the musty aroma of sand, pungent as wormwood or candlewax. The high peaks receded into the background, lofty above the lower range, a dull lavender in the afternoon haze, unreachable as stars.

"Looks like they stopped here for a smoke or a palaver," Ben said, pointing to the moil of tracks, the brown remnants of burnt quirlys, the pocked dirt where some had taken a piss, including the horses. And fresh horse apples littered the ground, their acrid fumes still rising in wisps of steam.

"Half hour ago, maybe."

"Mighty close," Ben said.

"We might catch up to 'em."

"You think so? Looky yonder."

Several yards farther on, John saw the

tracks all at tangents to the trail as if they had scattered like a covey of quail, each veering off in a different direction. They rode several yards and examined the tracks. Deep indentations showed where the horses had dug in their hind hooves, spurred to jump into a lope, then a gallop.

Five men riding hell bent for leather in five different directions.

"Old Dick must have scared the pants off'n 'em," Ben said with a chuckle.

"Yeah, they're scattered to the winds."

"You won't catch up to 'em now, less'n you want to wear out leather and founder our horses."

"We don't need to follow them, Ben. We know where they're going. Let's cut trail down to the creek and follow it to Pueblo."

"Good idea, Johnny. Gent and Dynamite are plumb tuckered. It's been a long day."

"And it ain't over yet."

Ben frowned. There was no real hurry now, but he could have used some shade and a rest. He was plumb tuckered, too. The strain was not so much from riding, but from reading tracks and watching John Savage, with that look of the hunter on his face, that grim jaw set of determination as if he were some kind of marauding adventurer bent on laying waste to every living thing in his path. It was plain that John was on a mission, bent on vengeance, his heart throbbing at a murderous pace.

It was too bad, Ben thought, that young John had to grow up so fast. And before the day was done, much to Ben's regret, Johnny was going to have to grow up a little more, a little faster. He had been keeping the secret inside him so long, he felt as if he were going to burst open with it and splash it all over Johnny like a bucket of slop. But best to tell him now, out in the big emptiness of the foothills where John couldn't hurt anybody much, including himself.

They rode out of the valley and up onto a ridge where they looked down on more hills, rumples in the earth, gentle and rolling, dotted with trees and cactus, aspen along a small creek, their leaves fluttering in the breeze like green butterflies, their trunks looking as if whitewash had been painted over the brown, just slapped on with an erratic brush.

Ben felt a queasiness in his stomach. Soon, he knew, they would come to Fountain Creek and head south to Pueblo. A day's ride, maybe. Not long. And then they'd be in the city. It would be too late to tell Johnny then. He would take the bit in his teeth and dash straight for the cantina.

And he might be shot down without ever drawing that lethal silvered pistol of his.

They were starting down the slope when Ben cleared his throat. He had said the words many times, over and over in his mind. But when it came to uttering them, they all vanished and got jumbled and tossed out of order, so that he found himself searching for the easy phrases he had imagined, groping for the right words that he had formed so many times in his head.

"Johnny, ah, something you oughta know," Ben said. "Before we get there."

"Before we get where?"

"Well, I mean Pueblo. Or somewhere in Pueblo, damn it. Don't make me struggle to tell you what I got to tell you."

"Well, spill it then, Ben. What's on your mind that you can't just spit it out?"

"A lot, I reckon. Just keep quiet, will you, and let me get it out."

"All right."

"Remember when me, your daddy, and my brother Leland first come up here to prospect? You and your ma and little Alice stayed down in Taos with her brother and some folks we knew from back home."

"Yeah, I remember. I wanted to come with you, but Daddy wouldn't let me. He said I had to look after Ma and Alice. I was mad the whole time you all were gone."

"Well, and this is mighty hard to say, we kind of headquartered in Pueblo. We rode all over the mountains, and heard about Cripple Creek, rode up there and we all got the fever pretty bad. Then we found that stretch of creek, found some color and staked out our claims. Had to make several trips."

"I know all that," John said. "My pa went on and on about how you all prospected and found that stretch of creek. Daddy was mighty proud of what you all did."

"Well, yeah, and rightly so. But when we was all in Pueblo, we stayed at this little hotel on Calle Vaca. It was cheap and we got meals there. And right next door was a cantina where we could go and smoke and relax. You know."

"No, I don't know. What cantina?"

Ben knew that John's dander was up. He bristled like a cat spoiling for a fight, hair standing up on end, tail switching back and forth like a snake.

"Well, it was Rosa's Cantina, Johnny."

"Where Ollie's headed? The same one?"

"The very same, son. It's owned by Rosa Delgado, and if she ain't one of the prettiest Mexicans I ever laid eyes on, I don't know what."

"So?"

"So, your daddy and Rosa, they had eyes for each other. I mean, we was there by ourselves and it didn't seem like real life at night. There was music, Mexican music, and pretty women, and dancing, and all. And Rosa, she and your daddy, well, they had a fling I guess you'd call it. Wasn't nothin' more than that. But here's what you got to know, Johnny. We, me and your pa, saw Rosa a couple more times after we staked our claim and when we come down to the assay office and your pa was mighty proud of striking gold and he told Rosa and she, well, I think she was the one what told Ollie about your pa and where to find him."

Ben closed his mouth and looked at John.

John's face darkened with a sullen rage that he kept inside him. But the veins on his neck stood out like blue worms and his eyes narrowed down so much they didn't have any light in them. Yet he didn't explode or go into a rage. He just rode on, smoldering like some lighted fuse, or a banked fire, and Ben could feel it, could feel the knife going into Johnny's heart, could feel him twisting and squirming on its point as it burrowed deeper into him.

It was a hell of a thing to tell Johnny, but he had to know.

Rosa Delgado would not be friendly when she saw him and John walk into her cantina.

He was pretty sure that Ollie was going to pay her for the information she gave him. He was going to pay her in gold.

And the gold had Dan Savage's blood on it.

"Johnny," Ben said, after a while, as they topped still another ridge and could see the shadowy plain in the distance, the shadows from the low hills stretching out to it like desperate fingers, and there, shining like silver, Fountain Creek, its waters tumbling over rocks, shadows playing in the foam, making each one a winking eye. "I'm sorry."

And then John said the words Ben dreaded to hear, but knew were coming.

"I'll kill her," John said, and there wasn't a hint of anger or bitterness in his tone. He said the words so matter-of-factly, he might have been talking about buying something at the store, a stick of licorice, perhaps, a trinket for his sister Alice.

And, as the sun fell behind a cloud, there was a sudden chill over the land, and the breeze picked up as if the gods were whispering among themselves about what they had in store for certain mortals bound up in the terrible coils of fate.

17

John felt as if someone had slammed a pile driver straight into his stomach. What Ben had told him about his father came as a great shock to him. He could not picture his father with another woman. Nor could he come to grips with his father keeping a secret like that from his mother. What kind of a spell had this Rosa woman cast over Dan Savage? And why did she betray him?

A hundred questions flooded John's mind as he and Ben rode slowly down the slope into the shadowy cut between two swollen hills, a narrow ravine that still bore traces of the rain. The rocks were wet and slippery and their horses made mud out of the damp soil, their hooves sinking deep at times, making sucking sounds as Gent and Dynamite lifted their hooves, breaking the seal.

They came out of the draw and crossed one of the outlaw tracks. The sign showed that the rider was still running, pushing his horse. Flung dirt littered the ground where the animal had passed. John studied the hoofprints carefully and reasoned that Ollie was not the horseman, and he didn't know which of the men had made them. All he knew, for sure, was that neither Dick nor Ollie were on that particular animal.

"We'll not make the creek today," Ben said, looking ahead at other hills that rose up before them.

"No matter. We've got plenty of water and we can chew on jerky and hardtack some more, I reckon. I'm not going to wear out our horses chasing this one."

"First thing you've said lately's made any sense, Johnny."

"Well, the way these men are scattered, we'll beat something of them into Pueblo. Ollie's the one I want most."

"The big feller."

"Yeah, the leader."

"Can you kill five more men, Johnny? There's the law, you know."

"The law?"

"You could swear out a warrant for them in Pueblo. Have them arrested for murder."

"I could tie sewing thread to bumblebee's legs and fly 'em like kites, too."

"You don't think the law would hang those men for what they done?"

They rode in deep shadow, the sun already dipped behind the highest peaks. The flat was laced with old sheep trails, narrow paths less than a foot wide.

"Look yonder," Ben said, "over where them aspens is growing. Looks like a tank."

John saw the land slope off near the white-boned trees and what looked like a dirt bank beyond an even deeper depression.

"Horses can water there, if the tank's holding some," John said.

"That makes it easy."

"I got a feeling about that fellow who took to the slope," John said. "Something we might do when we make camp."

"He might be up there looking down at us now," Ben said, glancing up at that last low hill with its long ridgeline.

"I'm counting on it," John said.

A few gilded clouds streamed like salmon on the sky and there was still that faint afterglow tingeing the blue with a coppery fringe. It was more than a little chilly, even with the extra clothes they were wearing, and the two men began to shiver.

They came to a grove of aspen where the ground was fairly dry. The horse tracks were no longer visible. They had turned off to the east, toward that last foothill, and John had decided not to follow it. He'd had enough fighting for one day, and whoever was on that horse could be waiting up at the top to pick them off. He'd have the advantage. He and Ben would be riding blind up a slope that had already darkened near to night.

"I'd bet that Ollie will already have an alibi set up. It would be our word against his," John said.

"You mean that woman. Rosa Delgado."

"Yeah, I mean Rosa Delgado. You know her. Would she lie for Ollie and his men?"

They stopped in the grove of aspen. The horses whickered gently, softly. The leaves jiggled in the breeze like scraps of green bunting. Water rippled in the tank. The horses whickered at the smell of the water. Beyond, there were more trees, and some open spots, small glades where they could spread their bedrolls and still have some protection. The shadows deepened, distorting all the landmarks and the trees, turning some into hostile, threatening shapes that tricked the eyes. They pulled their rifles from their sheaths and walked back to the tank.

Then, sudden nightfall, as the sun died in the west, taking the last glowing coals with it. They threw down their bedrolls, let the horses slake their thirst with a snuffling of lips, a snorting through rubbery nostrils, and a siphoning through their teeth. Then they led the animals, still saddled, some distance away into a lush, thick grove of small pines, hobbled them, tied them to lariats so they could graze on the plentiful grass.

"Why so far away, Johnny?"

"We're going to pitch two camps, make one fire," he said, laconically. "Get out your knife."

"My knife? What for?"

"You taught me something that first night," John said. "When we cut those spruce boughs. We're going to do some tree trimming here. Try not to make a whole lot of noise."

"You are a caution, young Savage," Ben said.

"Wait'll you see how cold that ground's going to be, old man."

Puzzled, Ben helped John lay out one camp. They collected stones, made a fire ring, gathered deadwood and squaw wood, placed some of it in the center.

"We won't light it yet," John whispered. "Now, let's get to cutting."

The two trimmed some pine boughs, carried them over by the fire ring. John arranged some on the ground. When he finished, they stretched the length of a man.

Then he threw his blanket over it.

Ben, without being told, did the same to another spot. When they stepped back, the blankets resembled two sleeping figures.

"Where we goin' to sleep?" Ben asked.

"About twenty yards away, behind that jumble of rocks."

"I can't see ten feet. What jumble of rocks?"

John chuckled and led Ben over to a pile of stones on a small knoll. They cleared spaces, removing most of the small stones and sticks.

"We'll freeze our asses off," Ben said.

"Might not have to stay here that long."

"Oh?"

"We'll see," John said. "Now, go down there and light that fire. When it gets going, come on back. I'll sit here with my rifle."

"You using me as bait?"

"Just get the fire going, and make it high."

Ben knelt down, struck a match, touched it to the squaw wood. Flames licked at the smaller sticks. The air pockets exploded in sporadic pops and the flames got higher. Ben added more wood, set heavier pieces on both sides. When he walked away, he glowed a warm peach color as the flames reflected off his clothing and skin. When he got to where John was waiting, he sat down, picked up his rifle and gazed down at the fire. The campsite looked like two men were sleeping nearby. The water in the tank reflected the flames so that the orange glow could be seen from a great distance, even to the summit of that last foothill.

"Now, we wait," John said, jacking a cartridge into the chamber of his rifle, then easing the hammer back down to half cock.

Ben did the same with the Henry, then set it on the ground beside him.

"If I was a bandit," Ben said. "That sure would look tempting."

"Better dig into your saddlebags and put some grub in that growling stomach of yours," John said.

Ben sighed. "Good idea."

Every so often, either Ben or John would steal down to the fire and feed it more dry wood. The flames danced and spewed swirling troupes of golden fireflies into the night, as if someone slept close by and was tending it. And then John told Ben to get some shut-eye, that they would put no more wood on the fire and just let it burn down as if its tenders, warm from its heat, and weary from travel, had fallen asleep.

Fritz Schultz had seen the two riders marking his trail, following his horse's tracks onto the meadow that butted up against that last hill. He had pushed his tired horse up it, clear to the top and over on the other side where he had a clear view of Fountain Creek and the plain beyond. He slid from the saddle, ground-tied his dun mare, and crept back to the crest of the hill with one of his rifles, a Sharps .50 buffalo gun he had stolen in Kansas.

He had killed the man who owned the rifle, an ex-cavalryman who had ridden with Quantrill's Raiders, then become a hide hunter after the war, and retired to live out his days in peace. The Big Fifty, as Fritz called it, was deadly accurate, had a smooth action, and killed anything it was aimed at. He crawled to a soft bare spot and watched the two riders head into the aspen trees where they watered their horses at an old sheep tank. His heart was pounding as he waited for them to come out and get back on his trail.

But they didn't come out, and later, he saw the flicker of a fire when it was full dark and the stars sprinkled across the sky like diamonds. When he looked real hard, he thought he saw the two men sleeping under blankets near the fire.

Still he waited, his body chilled by the cold ground and the high wind that brushed across the top of the hill, carrying in its freshets the coolness of white snow atop the high peaks that shone like distant ghosts under the soft alabaster light of the rising moon.

Fritz rubbed his eyes and bit off a chew of tobacco to ward off his sleepiness. He watched as someone fed the fire fresh wood, wondering how long those two would stay awake as he continued to watch the moon rise slowly, dusting the meadow with dull pewter, blaring down at him like some gaunt, cold, all-seeing eye.

And finally he saw the fire die down, saw it shrink to glowing orange embers, and he heaved a sigh of relief. He touched the extra cartridges in his pocket, within easy reach. The Sharps was a single shot, but he could load almost as fast as a man with a lever-action repeater. And he had confidence in the killing power of the .50-caliber soft lead slug. Such a bullet would tear a hole in a man big as a baby's fist, and smash through bone as if slicing through paper.

He got to his feet and walked downslope at an angle, careful to make no noise. He kept the dying fire in view as he traversed the hill, descended lower. He stopped every so often and listened to the deep quiet of the night. He rubbed his eyes again and again. He chewed on the plug, and bit off another. The tobacco bit into his mouth and throat, helped keep him awake and alert.

In the distance, a wolf howled, and another picked up its crooning call. Fritz froze and listened. He was close to the sleeping men. Another hundred yards should bring him so close he could not miss, even in the dark. He could still see the glowing sparks of the coals, winking bright and fading in the surge of the restless, sniffing breeze.

The wolves went silent, and Fritz stepped closer to the two hulks on the ground. His heart sped up, and his finger caressed the trigger of the Sharps. His thumb sweated on the hammer, oiling it with a thin film of moisture.

"You will not see me," Fritz whispered in the silence of his mind. "You will never know what hit you, boys. You will hear only a last explosion and then you will sleep on, forever."

He built up his courage with these and other bolstering phrases. He crept still closer, going more slowly, testing every footfall before he put his full weight on his boot heel.

The aspen stood like blanched signposts, their leaves whispering in the soft caress of the steady breeze blowing down from the mountains. It was so quiet, Fritz could hear his careful breathing, could hear his heart throbbing in his temples, beating in his chest.

Close, and ever closer, he tiptoed, his thumb on the hammer growing heavy, his finger on the trigger rubbing off its sweat until the metal was as slick as a skinned willow branch.

He stopped, stood looking at the two blanketed mounds. Neither moved. He took another step, halted, rubbed his eyes again. He brought the rifle to his shoulder, raised it so slowly it might have been a feather. He snugged the butt into his shoulder and sighted down the barrel at the farther blanket.

He pulled in a breath and held it. The gun barrel steadied. He pulled the hammer back quickly and fired so fast, its click was nearly drowned in the explosion. Fiery sparks and white smoke belched from the muzzle. Fritz worked the action, levering the chamber open. The spent shell ejected, flickered in the corner of his eye like some maddened insect spinning to the ground. He slid another cartridge into the chamber, levered up and swung the barrel on the nearer blanket. He fired without thinking, knowing his aim was true.

He heard a crackle of something breaking

and he did not fish another cartridge from his pocket, but stepped closer to see if both men were dead.

He heard something else, then. At first he thought it might be a deer, startled from its bed, or rousted from a feeding place in the aspen grove. He heard the crack of small branches and then saw something dark rushing toward him. Something black and deadly, coming so fast he thoughtlessly let his rifle fall from his hands as he clawed for the pistol on his hip, knowing he would have to kill whatever it was at close range.

And then Fritz saw something flash above the onrushing figure just before it pounced on him. Something shiny and silvery in the moonlight, like a single beam descending on him just as his fingers tightened around the grip of his pistol.

He cried out, but it was too late.

He knew, in that instant, that he had made a terrible mistake.

The lump of tobacco froze in his mouth, its juices trickling down his throat, blocking off his scream of terror.

18

John barreled into the outlaw. He slashed downward with his knife, aiming at Fritz's right arm. He felt the knifepoint strike flesh and bone even as his momentum jolted his body into Fritz's, knocking him backward.

Fritz screamed in pain as the knife cut into his wrist. His hand released its grip on his pistol and he drew it toward his midsection. His back slammed into an aspen with sickening force as blood streamed from his wound. Lights exploded in his brain as the back of his head slammed against the tree.

John raised his knife to strike again. Fritz slammed a fist into John's chest and pushed, knocking him back a half foot. John watched Fritz slide away from the tree while he grabbed for the handle of his own knife. In a half crouch, Fritz pulled his knife from its sheath, then swiped it back and forth as he stood up, then hunched over into a fighting stance.

John crouched, too, holding his knife out in front of him, looking for an opening. The two men circled, stalking each other, as Ben emerged out of the darkness, pistol in hand.

"Stay out of it Ben," John husked. He was breathing hard from the excitement and exertion, but he was not winded.

"Just in case," Ben said laconically.

Fritz thrust his knife out, trying to jab John in the belly. John flexed his gut, tucking it in tight, then chopped downward. His knife blade grazed Fritz's arm as he jerked it back out of the way. A tiny trickle of blood oozed from a razor-thin cut.

Fritz paid no attention to Ben. His gaze held on John and his knife. He weaved back and forth as if enticing John to come at him. John blew out a breath, then breathed back in as if gathering strength in him to rush the outlaw. He feinted with his knife and Fritz bobbed his head like a boxer, made a short jab toward John.

"Watch him, Johnny," Ben said quietly, duplicating John's motions, feinting and dodging first one way, then the other, like a spectator at ringside.

Fritz was like a cornered animal. He knew he was going to die. If this Johnny didn't kill him with his knife, the old man was standing ready to shoot him with his gun.

Either way, he was a dead man. But he might be able to do in the kid. A bullet was preferable to getting knifed in the gut.

John relaxed, as if he were going to give up the fight. He took a step backward. He held the knife pointed at Fritz, as if waiting for the outlaw to make a move. Fritz held to his crouch and raked his knife back and forth as if gauging the distance for a thrust, or looking for just the right opening.

"Well, come on, Johnny boy," Fritz said. "You gonna fight or just stand there?"

"Which one are you?" John asked.

"Huh?"

"Your name. What's your name?"

"Fritz. Fritz Schultz. Why? What difference does it make?"

"I just wanted to make sure your name fit your face."

"You fooled me once, Johnny boy. You ain't foolin' me again. Come on. Make your move."

"Be careful, Johnny," Ben said and took a step backward.

"Yeah, Johnny boy, be real careful," Fritz said.

John looked at Fritz's eyes. He remembered his face, the look on it when he had killed up at their claim. The man had ice for blood. He had shown no emotion as he blew

Donny French's brains out. Just a smirk of satisfaction on his weasel face.

Fritz's eyes shifted back and forth in their sockets. He licked his lips. John dropped his right shoulder and that drew a response from Fritz.

Fritz bunched his muscles, leaped from his crouch, and charged straight at John. He made a low animal sound in his throat, rammed the knife toward John's belly.

John seemed to uncoil. One moment he seemed completely at ease, the next he was all muscle, lean as a whip, springing into action.

He slashed high and he slashed low. Fritz stabbed at empty air. Then John stepped in with a wide swipe of his knife, cutting across Fritz's belly with the tip and then six inches of steel blade that opened a cut so deep that blood spurted from the wound like a crimson fountain. Fritz staggered backward, unsteady on his feet.

Ben hunched forward, eyes glittering.

Fritz groaned and dropped his knife in the dirt. He clutched his belly with both hands. Blood painted his fingers, flowed to his wrists. There was the smell of a severed intestine. He dropped to his knees, wide-eyed, a look of surprise on his face. John stepped in, kicked Fritz's knife away, knocked his hat off and grabbed a handful of hair, jerked the man's head back, exposing his throat.

John held the knife poised above Fritz's throat. His jaw tightened as he clamped his teeth together, nearly consumed with rage and the instinct to finish off his enemy, to slaughter him as Fritz had slaughtered Donny.

"Finish it," Fritz rasped. "Damn you, boy, finish it."

"I want you to die real slow, Fritz. I want you to think about what you done to my people, to my pa and ma, my little sister."

"I didn't kill that little girl. You know I didn't."

"You killed her. You take the blame for all of them, you sonofabitch."

The wound in Fritz's stomach widened. A bubble of intestine poked out, protruded like some hideous growth.

John pulled hard on Fritz's hair, jerked his head back even farther. He pushed the point of his knife into the flesh right into the Adam's apple. A tiny drop of blood oozed out. John let out a long sigh.

He thought of Alice and his mother. Their faces flashed in his brain and then vanished. Tears welled up in his eyes. He wanted to kill this man. He wanted to cut his throat and watch his blood spurt out like his father's and the others'. He wanted Fritz to suffer greatly during his last seconds of life.

Disgusted with himself, with his raging emotions, John spat and flung Fritz's head to the side and stepped back.

"How long do you think it'll take you to die, Fritz?" John said in a breathy whisper. "How long?"

Fritz keeled over to one side. He drew his legs up in agony. His belly wound opened wider and more intestine oozed out, pouring its stench into the crisp night air.

Ben walked over, picked up Fritz's pistol and the Sharps. He stuck the pistol inside his belt, held the Sharps up to look at it.

"He come to do business, looks like," Ben said.

"Stoke up that fire, will you, Ben?"

"Sure. Won't take much. Coals still hot."

Ben brought the fire back to life. The flames scrawled liquid shadows and ochre waves across Fritz's face. Ben warmed his hands over the fire after laying the Sharps down and holstering his pistol. John wiped the blade of his knife on his trousers and slid it back in its scabbard. He continued to watch Fritz, who opened and closed his eyes, wheezed air through his mouth that sounded like someone squeezing a toneless accordion.

John hunkered down next to Fritz, while Ben tickled the fire with a willow stick to keep it stirred up. He sat next to it, close enough to see both Fritz and John and hear every word they said.

"Fritz, can you talk some?" John asked, his voice strangely pitched, sounding almost kindly.

"What about?"

"I want to know about Rosa Delgado," John said.

"Rosie? What about her?"

"She sweet on Ollie?"

Fritz started to laugh and choked on his breath. He went into a spasm and Ben thought that might be the end of him, but he recovered and gazed up at John with red-rimmed eyes glazed over like Christmas caramel apples.

"Ollie's put the dally on her, if that's what you mean," Fritz said. "Him and Rosie are going to get married and start a new life out in Californy."

"That so," John said. "They know each other a long time?"

"A long time, yeah. Ollie staked her in the cantina business. Back in '88. Met her in Taos, in '87, brung her to Pueblo right about then."

John didn't say anything for several moments. He appeared to be thinking about what Fritz had told him, trying to piece together why his own father had taken up with the Mexican woman.

"Pretty, is she?" John said.

"Who? Rosie? Yeah, she's pretty as a flower. Wears red ones in her hair. Eyes that melt a man's heart. Legs of a thoroughbred out of Kentucky. Yeah, she's pretty all right. How come you want to know about her?"

"How come she and my father, Dan Savage, got in the blankets?"

"You're Dan's kid? Well, don't that beat all."

"You knew him?"

"I seen him a time or two. He was sparkin' Rosie all right. Didn't mean nothin' to her. That was Ollie's doin'."

"You don't say," John said.

"Well, this Dan come down with all this gold and braggin' about a strike up in Cripple Creek, so Ollie took notice. Hell, we all did."

"And so Rosa Delgado became Dan's friend."

"Hell, he didn't have no chance. Pretty woman like that breathing smoke in his ear, runnin' her fingers through his hair. Dan was a goner the minute he walked into that cantina. Yeah, too bad. I think maybe Ollie was the one who shot your pa. Kind of paying him back for the liberties Dan took with Rosie."

John shook his head and drew in a deep breath as if he were trying not to cry, not to think about his father with that treacherous woman.

"I ain't sayin' no more," Fritz said, and tried to wriggle on his back so that his guts would stop falling out.

Ben poked at the fire, kept his head down so that he wouldn't have to look at John, see how miserable he was, hearing all that from Fritz Schultz.

Without a word, John got to his feet and walked away, disappearing into the darkness. Ben watched him go, thinking he probably had gone to relieve himself. Then he heard a stirring in the brush, and a few moments later, John appeared on horseback, riding Gent. He rode up to Frtiz, pulled his lariat from the saddle and dismounted. As Ben watched, John built a loop and slipped it over Fritz's boots.

"What are you doing, John?" Ben asked.

"I don't want this bastard stinking up our camp. You just sit tight. I'll be back."

Fritz looked up, saw his feet rise in the air as John mounted Gent and took up the slack in the rope.

"What's goin' on?" Fritz said.

"You're going for a little ride, Fritz."

"You goin' to drag me?"

"That's right. You can think about what you and Ollie and your brother outlaws did to my family and all the others up on Cripple Creek. You can look up at the stars and say your last prayer, you sonofabitch."

John ticked Gent's flanks with his spurs and Fritz's body jerked from where it had lain. Fritz put out his hands to stop himself, but all he did was burn his palms with rocks. John put Gent into a gallop and Fritz screamed. He kept on screaming for several moments as Ben stared after the two men, his mouth opened in abject bewilderment.

Ben could hear the bouncing body for some time as it tore over rocks and bounced against trees. He closed his eyes and tried not to think about it.

After a while, John rode back, his rope coiled up neat and attached to his saddle. He rode back to where Dynamite was tethered and soon joined Ben by the fire. He sat down and stared into the fire, then looked away.

"Johnny, you make me wonder," Ben said.

"Yeah? About what?"

"About what makes your clock tick, son.

What you did to that man. He was wounded bad and you dragged him. He dead?"

"Yeah, he's dead. That leaves only four."

"You get any satisfaction out of what you just done?"

"Not in particular, no. I killed a snake, dragged him away from our camp, that's all."

"You got a mean streak in you what wasn't there before, Johnny."

"I guess everybody's got one, to some degree or another."

"Not civilized folk."

"If Ollie and that bunch are examples of civilized folks, that's mighty pitiful, Ben."

"You don't have to go down to their level."

"Maybe I do."

"No, Johnny. You got to get a hold of yourself. You're turning into a savage."

John chuckled.

"I was born a Savage," he said.

"You know what I mean."

"Yeah, I know what you mean. What those owlhoots took away from me I can never get back. But they don't deserve to live. I keep thinking of poor little innocent Alice. She's gone and they took her. You try getting over something like that, Ben."

"Vengeance is mine, sayeth the Lord, Johnny."

John was silent for a long time. Beyond the last foothill, they heard a coyote yapping, followed by a chorus of others. Then the yaps changed to a melodic chorus, trilling calls that traversed up and down the scale like bright ribbons floating on the night air, unearthly, haunting, as if the hounds of hell had suddenly been unleashed upon the world.

The sounds faded as the coyotes chased whatever they were chasing.

It was quiet, with only the soft crackling of the flames nibbling on dry wood, to punctuate the private thoughts of Ben and John, who spoke no more that night and finally turned in, grabbing their blankets up and rolling themselves in them to stave off the chill that would descend upon them before morning.

19

Ollie Hobart didn't like being alone. He was used to having hard men around him, men he could trust to watch his back, men he could count on when the proverbial chips were down. Now he rode within sight of Fountain Creek, the sun painting the waters with streamers of gold and silver, burnt umber, ochre, touches of viridian from the aspen leaves that shone like green fire on the limbs of the trees.

Red Dillard was the first to ride up. Ollie saw him come down the slope of a hill, descend into a fold of land, and emerge on the flat. His horse, a bay mare, looked worn out, and when he caught up to Ollie, Red's skin was twitching beneath his eye as if some formless inchworm was working its way across part of his face underneath the skin.

"You get any shut-eye, Red?" Ollie asked. He had an unlit cheroot in his mouth, had chewed the end into a shapeless mass.

"Not much. You?" His blue eyes shifted back and forth, making the twitch on his face even more pronounced.

"I slept on my horse until just before the crack of dawn. I swear, what with the coyotes and the wolves a-howlin' half the night, I just couldn't keep my eyes closed for more than a few minutes at a time.

"Any sign of the others?"

Ollie shook his head.

He looked back up the creek, saw nothing.

"You got a lucifer, Red?" Ollie held up the cheroot.

Red dug out a box of matches, struck one, and lit the end of the cheroot. Ollie pulled on it, getting very little smoke. He bit off the chewed end, spat it out, and tried again. The smoke filled his mouth.

"We goin' to wait here for the others?" Red asked.

"They know the meetin' place. Let's ride on."

"Now I see why you kept all the gold, Ollie. No tellin' where everybody else is. I'm stickin' with you."

Ollie chuckled and puffed his cheroot. They continued along the road that bordered the creek. A black-and-white magpie landed on the opposite bank, strutted alongside until it found a suitable place to drink. It flapped its wings, dipped its beak into the water, withdrew it quickly, and shook its head. Another magpie flew down, landed next to it, and began squawking. The two birds argued for a minute and then the first magpie flew off, landed in a cotton-wood, sputtering invective.

"Yonder comes old Army," Red said, pointing to a shallow draw where a rider had just emerged.

Ollie watched Mandrake negotiate the brush. His hat brim was pulled low to block out the rays of the low sun.

"His horse looks tuckered," Ollie said.

"It's hell bein' chased."

"Chased by a damned kid," Ollie griped.

"And an old man."

"Army can take care of him," Ollie said.

Red laughed. Army was the oldest among them, and they all joked about that. Behind Army's back; never to his face.

The two men waited for Army to ride up. He wore a worn corduroy vest over a woolen shirt the color of olive drab. The vest was covered with dirt, and so were his duck trousers. He touched a finger to his hat in greeting.

"Army," Ollie said. "With that face you're

wearin' you got to be the bearer of bad news."

"We ain't goin' to see Schultzie no more, Ollie. Found him on the other side of that hill back yonder, deader'n a doornail." He cocked a thumb in the direction of the hill some two miles or so distant.

"Shot?" Red said.

"Didn't see no bullet holes in him. Found his head about two hunnert yards away. He was cut up pretty bad, his guts strewn out for nigh a mile, a big slash in his belly. Didn't see no bullet hole in his head, neither."

Ollie swore. "So, he didn't just fall of his horse and get dragged," Ollie said.

Army shook his head. He spit out a stream of tobacco juice and shifted the cud to the other side of his mouth. His face was furrowed with deep lines, and these were caked black with grime so that he looked like he was wearing a cut-down version of war paint.

"No, and that's another thing," Army said. "I found his horse, and tracks of two others up on the sunny side of that foothill yonder. Them two miners come up and shot that horse in the head. Looks like they used Fritz's Big Fifty to put the horse down and then just threw the rifle down next to him."

"Was Fritz still wearing his pistol?" Ollie asked.

Army shook his head.

"Nope. And his blade was gone, too. Looks like he got in a knife fight with them two miners."

"Fritz was good with a knife," Red said. "And mean with a knife."

"Well, I didn't see the other feller," Mandrake said, "but Fritzie was cut up in his hand pretty bad and gutted like a Red River catfish. Gave me the pure-dee willies."

"Let's get on to Pueblo," Ollie said. "Hell, them two miners could be most anywhere. You boys keep your eyes peeled right sharp, hear?"

Less than an hour later, they saw Dick Tanner waiting for them up ahead, flapping his arms back and forth like he was sending semaphore signals. When they rode up on him, his face was bone white, and it was plain he'd washed some of the dirt off in the creek.

"What the hell's the matter with you, Dick?" Ollie asked.

"I tell you, Ollie, I was plumb spooked all night, thinkin' about that kid and that fancy pistol of his. I rode around in circles half the night, come up on a she-bear and her pair of cubs and she liked to scare the shit out of me. Take a look at Bessie's hind end."

The three men looked at the steeldust gray's rump. Raw flesh showed on three deep gouges more than half a foot long.

"Bear did that?" Red said.

"Bessie liked to run out from under me. She caught its scent, but it was too late. Them two cubs come tumblin' out of the brush and Bessie shied. Never saw the she-bear until we heard it roar and come out of nowhere on all fours. She jumped at Bessie. Bessie scooted, but that bear's claws caught her and that horse screamed, whooeee, I tell you."

"You get any sleep?" Ollie asked.

"Nope. I was too busy gettin' lost."

"And gettin' chased by a bear," Mandrake said, drily. "You really know how to live, don't you, Dick?"

"You can poke all the fun you want, Army, but you wasn't in my boots. I kept hearin' brush crashin' and twig's poppin' and I swear them two jaspers was doggin' me half the night."

"No, they weren't," Ollie said. "They were too busy putting Fritz's lamp out."

"Fritz?" Tanner's face lost another shade or two of pink. He was beginning to look like someone who had fallen into a trough of whitewash.

"Yeah," Dillard said. "Fritz bought the cotton-pickin' farm, Dick."

"I told you," Dick said. "That kid's unnatural as all get out. He's got that look, you know?"

"What look, you peckerhead," Ollie said, losing patience.

"I don't know, Ollie. He's got that look a preacher gets when he's talkin' about sin and damnation. He's got the look a snake oil drummer gets when he's got an old crippled woman up and walkin' when the docs have give up. You know, that goddamned look."

"Let's get the hell to Pueblo," Ollie said. "Tanner, you better take some of that snake oil and get rid of them heebie-jeebies you got in your yellow belly."

Dick reared back as if he had been slapped in the face with a rug duster. If his face had been pale before it was now almost as white as a linen sheet.

The four riders stepped out, heading south for Pueblo. And three of them kept looking back over their shoulders. Only Ollie kept his eyes straight ahead, a determined glint in his eye. Every so often, he'd look up into the hills, but his mind was on one thing: getting to Pueblo and seeing Rosa Delgado again.

A small herd of pronghorn galloped across the plain. A lone sentinel stood like a garden statue watching the four riders, his white throat shining bright in the sun, his ebony horns adorning him like a stately crown. Small iron-red buttes dotted the land, golden outcroppings of rocks, mesas like giant ships in the background, shimmering under the wriggling shawls of heat waves. Turkey buzzards floated in the sky on invisible carousels, their wings outstretched, the tips just tickling the sky every so often.

They passed through the dusty, nondescript settlement of Fountain, almost without notice. A Mexican, sitting in the shade, his sombrero tipped low over his face, looked up and then went back to dozing. A few slat-ribbed dogs slunk into adobe shadows, and a large woman with a load of wash in a wicker basket waddled out of their way, two brown-skinned urchins tagging along after her with a hoop and sticks, their brown eyes too big for their little black-haired heads.

"You see anything back there, Army?" Ollie asked when they were an hour further south. "You keep lookin' like you're expectin' your mother-in-law."

"Hard to tell. Might be specks in my eyes. Might be a couple of riders."

"Anybody got field glasses?" Ollie asked.

"I think Pete had 'em last," Red said.

"Shit," Ollie said and, for the first time, he looked back up the road. His horse jounced him so much it was difficult to focus, but after several seconds of looking, he swung his head back around.

"I don't see anything at all," he said. "Even if they was to come up on us, it's four against two."

"That kid, that Savage kid," Dick said, "is faster'n greased lightning with that six-gun of his."

"Fast don't make straight," Army said. "Fast don't make true."

"Well, this kid shoots fast and true," Dick said.

"He's really got you buffaloed, ain't he, Dick?" Red said, with a throaty chuckle. "Hell, he's just a kid. He'll stop a bullet same as anybody."

"You stop him, then, Red, you're so fucking smart." Some of the color had returned to Dick's face, but it might have been the burnishing sun falling off to the west, hitting him at just the right angle.

"It would be my great pleasure," Red said.

"Trick is," Ollie said, "don't never look at his gun. Look the bastard square in the eyes. It's that fancy gun's got you spooked, Dick.

Take off all the glitter, it's still just a Colt six-shooter. You pack one yourself."

"The one that kid's packin' has eyes," Dick said.

Army and Red laughed.

Ollie just screwed his face up into a sullen frown. He was tired of hearing about the Savage boy. It was just dumb luck that he had killed the others. Or, they had just gotten stupid, dropped their guards.

Ahead in the distance, smoke scrawled across the sky, smoke from the smelters in Pueblo. It twisted and turned in the high currents like something alive, the shadow of a snake, or streamers of dark bunting. It contrasted against the golden cloud bunnies that flocked the sky over the plains and clear up to the mountains.

Ollie's heart picked up a beat.

"There she is," he said. "El Pueblo, a mean bastard of a town."

"Seems like home," Dick said. "I'm plumb sick of mountains."

Nobody said anything, they just looked up at the smoke, knowing there was a city underneath, and that meant a soft bed, a bath, a shave, some good whiskey, or mescal, or tequila, maybe a painted woman to warm the blankets, not a speck of wind inside a hotel room, and music to make the boards dance with the stomping of boots and long heels on shiny patent-leather shoes.

And the gold in Ollie's saddlebags. Pounds of yellow dust, waiting to be cashed in and split up. And now split only four ways.

"Rosie will be glad to see you, Ollie," Red said.

Ollie smiled. They still had a good five miles to go, just to the edge of the city. Another long ride to Calle Vaca and Rosa's Cantina.

And where in hell was that kid and the old man?

He looked back up the road. It was as empty as a bartop at five in the morning. Not a cart, a wagon, a walker, or a horse in sight.

If they came, the kid and the old man, it would not be right away. If they were back there, following them, it would be full dark by the time they rode into Pueblo. And by the time they made their way to Rosa's, he would be ready for them.

And so would Rosa herself, and that scattergun she kept behind the bar.

Four against two. No, make that five against two.

Rosa was a crack shot and she had arctic blood in her veins.

20

The horse didn't see it. And there was no warning. It dipped its head, pushed its lips toward a tuft of grass growing out of a small depression in the earth. It shifted the bit in its mouth. The bit clattered against its teeth, the metal making a sound like a handful of clicking dice.

The timber rattler, no more than a foot long, struck with the speed of thought. It sank its fangs in the soft flesh of the horse's muzzle, square between its nostrils. The horse, a blue roan, gelded, snapped its head up. The snake held on, pumping venom into its veins. The horse shook its head violently from side to side, flinging the snake a dozen yards. Blood oozed from two small holes in its muzzle. It whinnied in pain and pawed the ground.

A half dozen other snakes began to coil and shake their tails. The rattles made an ominous buzzing sound. The snakes, scattered in the grass alongside the horse, struck at its legs, striking above the hocks and fetlocks, shooting venom into the horse's veins again and again as they struck, recoiled, and struck once more. The roan, with its close-cropped mane and bobbed tail, kicked at the snakes and tried to run, but its hobbles kept it anchored to the spot where it had aroused a nest of snakes.

"You hear that, Ben?" John said as they topped the hill.

"Rattlers."

"More than one."

"Several. Sounds like a sawmill down there." Ben slid the Sharps across the pommel. John had wanted him to leave it where it lay back at their camp, but the rifle's lure was too much for Ben. There was something about the big .50, its legend, perhaps, or its clean lines, that made him want to keep it. John argued that it had been used to kill one of their fellow prospectors.

"It's just a gun. It don't have no brains," Ben said.

"No, but it has a history."

They rode down, and the rattling subsided. Now they could see the bobtailed roan twisting and kicking, stomping. As they rode close, they could see blood and what looked like pus oozing from several small holes in at least two of its legs.

"Would you look at that," Ben said in a breathy whisper.

The horse looked at them, its liquid brown eyes seemed to be pleading for help.

The horse began to turn in circles. Snakes hissed and slithered away to avoid its hooves. Then the horse lurched as it lost its step. It staggered to one side, tried to recover and staggered in the other direction.

"Snakebit, for sure," Ben said.

"That horse is plumb suffering," John said.

"Yeah. Must've got into a nest of rattlers. It won't last long."

"That's a terrible way to die, Ben."

"I reckon. Nothin' we can do about it though."

"We can put that horse out of its misery. That's what we can do."

Muscles on the roan's legs twitched. It seemed to lose control of which way its feet went. It emptied its bowels in steam and stench. Its hind legs bent and it tried to straighten them.

John grabbed the Sharps from Ben.

"Give me a cartridge for this."

Ben reached into his shirt pocket and handed John a .50-caliber cartridge. John pulled on the lever, opening the breech. He shoved the cartridge in, closed the breech, and took aim on the horse.

"Best thing you can do, Johnny."

John squeezed the trigger. The Sharps recoiled with the explosion. The bullet struck between the cinch and its right front leg, lifting a puff of dust before smashing through ribs into the horse's heart. It tried to rear up, standing on both hind legs. Then, it collapsed. One hind leg kicked out, the other quivered. There was only a small amount of blood as its heart stopped pumping. Muscles in its chest quivered reflexively, then went rigid and still. John rode in close and threw the Sharps down. The rifle landed on its butt, then fell across the horse's belly, the barrel resting against the stirrup.

"Perfectly good rifle," Ben said.

"Good riddance."

John turned his horse and headed down the slope toward the creek. Ben followed. He looked back longingly only once, then whapped Dynamite across the rump with the tips of his reins, putting the Sharps out of his mind. A moment later, he dipped into his shirt pocket and picked up the remaining two cartridges in there. He threw them, useless impedimenta now, onto the ground.

"Hell of a thing to have to put down a

sick horse," Ben said, as he caught up to John.

"You just sat there, watching it suffer."

"I don't think as quick as you, Johnny."

John turned to look at Ben. An angry shadow passed across his face.

"Do you even think at all, Ben?"

"That ain't fair."

"Maybe not fair, but true," John said. "Last night, you froze up when that bastard come after us in camp. Sat there like a damned toad."

"I ain't as quick as you, neither, Johnny. I mean, about killin'. I mean about killin' a man or a horse."

"There you go again, Ben. Bein' critical."

"Nope. Just commentin' on what's what."

"I was slow once. When those outlaws were killing everybody, I could have run down there, knocked one of them off his horse, taken his gun, and started fighting back. Might have saved my folks and my sister from gettin' killed. Might have saved a bunch of 'em."

"Johnny, them boys would have shot you to pieces before you ever got down them stairs."

That was probably true, John thought. He had gone over that scene so many times in his mind, wondering what might have happened if he had taken a pick and just slid down there into camp swinging it at the first killer he saw. He had created a number of scenarios that might have changed the outcome of the slaughter.

They were all fantasies, he knew, born of guilt that he was still alive and all the others were dead. Ben had probably saved his life by keeping him up at the mine, unarmed as they both were. Ben wasn't that slow, and he had shown wisdom in his decision to stay out of the fight. If they both had gotten into it, they would now be dead like all the others.

"I'm sorry, Ben. You don't deserve being caught up in my anger. I just boil over and can't help what I say to you sometimes."

"That's all right, Johnny. I understand. It eats at me, too. What might have been."

"Yeah. What might have been. Did Hobart have to kill everybody? Why couldn't he have just robbed them at gunpoint?"

"Maybe killin's his nature."

They ambled down the slope, tacking back and forth as if following some switchback trail. It was easier on the horses, put less strain on the saddle cinches. It was slower, but safer. John could smell the creek, and so could the horses. Their rubbery nostrils flexed as they sniffed the air. Their ears twisted, sometimes flattening, sometimes stiffening. This was new country for them and they were wary.

Just before they reached the flat, a jackrabbit exploded from cover and struck out for the creek. Both horses spooked, but Dynamite crashed through some rotten boards next to an old well. The sound spooked him even more, and he kicked at the boards, slashed at them with his front hooves, ripping through worm-eaten, weather-worn lumber hidden in the brush. He began to buck and Ben had his hands full trying to bring the horse under control. He held on to the saddle horn with his left hand, reined in hard with his right, bending the horse's head down until its muzzle almost touched its chest. Dynamite fishtailed and bounded stiff-legged over the scattered boards, stood on its front legs and kicked backward, its hooves striking empty air.

"Whoa, Dynamite, whoa," Ben shouted as the horse bucked on down to the flat before it stopped twisting and trying to throw Ben out of the saddle and off its back.

John had to fight Gent, but at least Gent didn't go into a bucking fit. The two watched the antics of Dynamite, through all of his gyrations. The dappled gray twisted, bit, kicked, and humped up like a scared cat until Ben brought the animal back under his control.

"That's one way to exercise your horse, Ben," John said, a trace of a smile on his lips. "I just walk mine with a halter."

"Ain't you the smart mouth, now, Johnny. That rabbit come out of nowhere. Scared the shit out of me, too."

"Well, the rabbit won that little race," John said. "By twenty lengths."

"Ha ha," Ben said, his face reddening with embarrassment and exertion. "You're real funny, Mr. Savage."

"All I can say is, you sure named that horse right, Ben. He come out of that brush like exploding dynamite."

John headed for the creek, knowing Gent was thirsty. When Ben didn't follow, he looked back.

Ben was leaning out from the saddle, looking down at Dynamite's legs. The horse was limping, favoring its left forefoot.

John turned Gent and rode up to Ben.

"Dynamite's gone lame, Ben."

"I know. Happened back there, when that rabbit jumped out."

"Let me take a look. Get down."

Ben dismounted. John did the same. He handed Ben the reins of his horse, knelt down next to Dynamite's left leg. He lifted its hoof. The horse held steady. John examined the shoe, saw a splinter sticking out. He touched it and the horse winced. The muscles in its leg quivered, rippling up and down its ankle.

"Going to have to take that shoe off, Ben. He's got a splinter in his hoof."

"That the only way you can get at it?"

"Looks like."

"Shit," Ben said.

"Can't be helped." John drew his knife from its sheath. Gingerly, he stuck the blade under the heel of the shoe, began to pry, moving the blade up and down gently to loosen it.

The horse tried to back away, pulling its sore hoof out of John's hand.

"Easy boy," Ben said. He rubbed Dynamite's muzzle to calm the horse.

"Hold him steady," John said. "I'll try it again."

He lifted the hoof. The shoe showed a small gap where he had pried it loose. He stuck the knife into the other side, pushed through the gap. He worked the blade, felt it strike one of the nails. He widened the gap, then moved the knife to the other side of both nails. He worked the knife down to the toe of the shoe, prying all the time. The nails loosened.

"Almost off," Ben said.

"Yeah. I think I can pull the shoe now."

John set the knife down, grabbed both sides of the shoe with his hand. He pulled up, straight toward him. The shoe came off, exposing the splinter of wood buried in the soft center of Dynamite's hoof. He dropped the shoe on the ground.

"This is going to hurt him a little," John said.

"I'll hold him."

Ben put his arm around Dynamite's neck. He spoke softly to the horse while John grabbed the splinter firmly with his thumb and index finger. He jerked on the end of the splinter. It came loose and the horse hopped away on the other foot.

"Got it," John said.

"All of it?"

"Yes, I think so."

"Can you put the shoe back on?"

John tried to hold the shoe to the hoof and insert one of the nails. The horse wouldn't stand for it, pulled its foot away.

"We need a blacksmith," John said. He stood up, handed the shoe and three nails to Ben.

"Damn," Ben said.

"We'll have to walk to Pueblo," John said, looking down the road.

"There's a little town called Fountain down the creek a ways. Maybe they have a blacksmith."

They watered their horses and set out down the road along the creek, walking the horses.

A pair of pintails ejected from the creek, rising straight up from an eddy at one of the bends, their graceful bodies shedding water droplets that burned amber in the sun. All along a stretch of grassy banks, mallards and green- and blue-wing teals took flight as Ben and John passed. The mallards quacked in protest, the whap-whap of their pinions sounding leathery in the hush of afternoon.

A muskrat swam upstream, a long stem of grass in its teeth, its wake blending the colors of the water into a flowing amalgam of subdued tints as the sun sank toward the snowcapped peaks in the distance. A line of hills began to turn purple and gray. A stately gray heron croaked and took flight like some ungainly specter of geometry that constantly changed shapes as it struggled to gain purchase on an invisible ladder of air.

The afternoon grew long shadows and gold burnished the rocky outcroppings on the plain, the small dark buttes in the distance, the craggy spires that jutted up like rocky minarets blasted by wind and rain into skeletal remnants of an ancient kingdom long since vanished from the earth.

The village of Fountain was half asleep when the two men entered the town to barking dogs, slinking cats, and the smells of corn tortillas and beans, hot lard, and cooking meat. Blessedly, they heard the ring of a hammer on an iron anvil, and the whickering burble of a horse, mingled with the bray of a donkey. They headed in that direction as their shadows puddled up at their feet and the sky glowed like Vulcan's workshop in the west, behind the dark towers of mountains, and the evening breeze turned chill as it blew against their weary faces. Lamps came on and lighted homely windows in adobe dwellings and brush-constructed jacales, chasing shadows with feeble orange light, and voices drifted from the huts in liquid scales of staccato Mexican.

It would be late in the evening, or early morning, John thought, before they could hope to reach Pueblo, even if they could re-shoe Dynamite and his lameness went away.

He cursed the lost time, but was helpless to do a damned thing about it.

A rooster crowed a scratchy madrigal from its sandpaper throat as the dusk descended

over Fountain and the black-water creek
that bore its name.

21

Rosa's Cantina on Calle Vaca was a large adobe structure that had once served as a mission when that part of the country was still claimed by Spain, and later, Mexico, until the United States took all the land between the Rio Bravo and the Rio Grande del Norte. It was in the old part of town, near the foothills, and near the main road to the mountains. It had survived the fire that destroyed much of El Pueblo, but the new city had largely forgotten its existence, partly because it was well off the beaten path, and partly because it catered to what the landed gentry now considered disreputable people.

Rosa kept her customers coming back because she served strong spirits at reasonable prices and she didn't cheat with watered-down drinks or serve up questionable whiskies such as Taos Lightning, whiskey that fried a man's brain and sometimes killed the drinker with impure alcohol. Rosa herself was an attraction, with her stunning good looks, attractive figure, and a personality that made every man feel welcome. Her girls didn't roll drunks nor pick their pockets, and her bouncers were not vicious thugs who hit first and asked questions later. They behaved more like regulators or peace officers, breaking up fights, calming hot tempers, and putting passed-out drunks to bed in one of the upstairs cribs until they sobered up.

But she was also an opportunist, and an information gatherer. When she learned that a customer had means, money, a mining claim, or a thriving business, she used this information for nefarious purposes. She might persuade a man needing money to follow up on this information and commit robbery, never anywhere near her cantina, nor shortly subsequent to a victim's visit, but sometime afterward. She would split the proceeds with whoever perpetrated the crime and add to her growing wealth. She was never suspected of any crimes, and none of her victims ever connected her to their misfortune. She stayed in the background. She kept her hands clean and her pretty mouth shut. And those who carried out her criminal wishes were fiercely loyal to her, for she could be counted on for bail money, bribes to officials in law enforcement, and even the hiring of a defense attorney when bribes failed. Rosa was a very smart woman, and she knew how to manipulate and control men. And, like many of those she used for her own purposes, she had absolutely no conscience whatsoever.

Rosa catered to the workers in the nearby smelters and to men riding the owlhoot trail. She was attracted to down-and-outers because she had come from humble beginnings herself, having grown up in bleak Sonora, the daughter of a poor farmer living on sixteen hectares of hardscrabble land. She had migrated to Texas where she worked as a cook for a rich family who treated her kindly and instilled in her a love of money and opulence.

When she was in her late teens, she ran off with an enterprising young man who was a trader in Santa Fe. He died of consumption and left her with enough money to journey north to Pueblo, where she bought the old, crumbling mission, restored it, and made herself living quarters above the cantina. She still had enough space left to construct cribs for the girls, and her charm brought in the customers, making the cantina a success even in that part of town.

She was sitting at the far end of the long bar when Ollie came in that night, saddlebags slung over his shoulders, rifle in hand, enough dust on him to create a small desert, and an unlit cheroot in his mouth. The Mexican musicians were on a break and the few diners were just finishing their meals. Oil lamps cast a homey glow on the tables, the small dance floor, and made the bartop gleam like flowing honey.

Rosa smiled, but did not leave her seat at the bar. She never chased men; they chased her.

Ollie smiled and walked slowly toward her, his gaze roving to the right and left, out of habit. A regular at the bar raised a hand in greeting when he recognized Ollie. Most of the other patrons ignored him.

"I can tell by the look on your face you had a successful trip," she said as Ollie stood next to her, a wide grin on his face. "Where are your compadres?"

"Puttin' up the horses. Good to see you, Rosa."

The stables a few doors down were another drawing card for the cantina, and there were three hotels on the same block. The one next door was the best of the three and had been where Dan Savage had taken a room when he was alive.

"Check in yet?"

"No. Wanted to see you first. Miss me?" He pulled out a stool, sat down.

"*Por supuesto, mi amor,*" she said.

"*Mi querida,*" he said.

Her black hair shone in the lamplight, polished ebony, tied up in a bun in back, a single blue flower pinned along one side. Her blue gingham dress was tied with a yellow sash, her sandals a pale pink. Just a touch of rouge on each cheek highlighted her high cheekbones, and her lips were moist, the red of rubies. She wore a pale blue choker around her graceful neck like a woman of culture and breeding. Her bracelet and rings were silver, inlaid with turquoise. The silver was from Tasco, but the jewelry was fashioned in Taos and sold in Santa Fe.

Ollie hungered for her and she knew it from the lustful gleam in his eye.

"You'd better take a cup," she said. "What is your pleasure?"

"Maybe you shouldn't ask that, Rosa."

She laughed, low in her throat, like a cat purring.

"You are horny, eh? Like the buffalo."

"Horny as a bull elk."

"And you smell like one, Ollie."

They laughed and she beckoned to the

bartender.

"I will buy you your first drink while you tell me all about your adventure. And maybe you will tell me what is in your saddlebags."

He pulled the bags from his shoulder and set them down between his feet. He shoed a boot toe under the flap.

"Pedro," Rosa said when the bartender appeared, "Mr. Hobart wishes a drink."

"*Buenas,* Mr. Hobart. Whiskey?" Pedro was thin, dark-skinned, wore a pencil-etched moustache, neatly trimmed side-burns, a white shirt with red garters.

"Pedro, you got any of that Old Taylor left back there?"

Pedro looked at Rosa. She nodded.

"Right away, Mr. Hobart."

Pedro poured two fingers of whiskey from an Old Taylor bottle into a shot glass.

One of the musicians struck a chord on his guitar. There was a shuffling of feet on the bandstand, a fluttering of sheet music on the stands.

Ollie picked up the glass, looked at Rosa.

"And for you, Rosa?"

"You know that I do not drink, Ollie."

"Not ever?"

"Never. Especially I would not drink when there is business to conduct with my lover."

They both laughed. Hobart drank half the

whiskey in the shot glass.

"There is business to conduct," Ollie said.

"You were successful then."

"Yeah, I guess so."

"You guess so? What does that mean? Was there not much, ah, what you went after?"

"We got plenty. Something else."

Her brows knit. Worry lines appeared on her forehead like small pencil marks.

"You must tell me, Ollie."

He told her about killing all the miners, the wife of Dan Savage, and their daughter. Rosa's eyes never blinked. Instead, they glowed in the lamplight like the feral eyes of a hunting cat, the pupils expanding and contracting with the telling of each detail.

"Did you know that Savage had a grown son?" Ollie asked.

"He mentioned this to me. Johnny, I think he was called."

"And, there was an old man we missed. I don't know his name."

"That would be Ben Russell. He drank here with Dan."

"Well, him and Johnny, or maybe just Johnny, killed four of my men and those two are breathing down our necks."

"Coming here?"

"Probably," Ollie said.

At that moment, the band struck up a

lively Mexican tune with lots of guitar runs, a cornet, and a drum. And Dick Tanner, Army Mandrake, and Red Dillard entered the cantina and marched to the bar near where Rosa and Ollie were sitting.

They looked at Ollie.

"Belly up, boys," he said, "and wet your whistles."

"Howdy, Rosie," Red said, touching a finger to his hat brim.

"Howdy," chorused Army and Dick as they each set a boot on the brass rail above the floor.

"They'll want their shares," Ollie said to Rosa.

"You have it all?" She expressed surprise.

"I kept it until we got here. Good thing, too."

"You want me to weigh it and give you cash?"

"If you can cover it."

Rosa smiled.

"And what about my share?" she said.

"Equal, of course."

She batted her eyes then, and they shone with excitement.

"You are a generous man."

"It's what we agreed on, Rosa."

"Yes. Is there a lot of money to divide?"

"Quite a bit, I reckon."

"You trust those men there? To keep quiet? To keep their money in their pockets and not boast about it?"

"I do," Ollie said. "They'll want to see the scales."

"Of course. I will buy their first drinks, too. But what are you going to do about Johnny Savage and Ben Russell? I do not want a shooting here in my cantina."

"I don't know. That kid is dangerous. He shot some good men. He's got him a fancy pistol and knows how to use it."

"We cannot let him come to the cantina, Ollie. You must take care of this business somewhere else."

Ollie glanced at the bat-wing doors. The music nearly drowned out all thought. A fiddle joined in, with its high whine, and the players tapped their feet on the wooden floor of the bandstand. Ollie finished off his drink, downing it in a single swallow.

"I may not have a choice, Rosa. That kid and the old man got real close. I been lookin' over my shoulder all damned day. They ought to be right behind us. They could walk through them doors at any moment."

Rosa's face registered alarm. Her eyebrows flared up, arching like a pair of caterpillars and her nose crinkled.

"That must not happen," she said.

"I'll send Red or Army outside to keep a lookout after we divide the *dinero*."

"You'd better send two men," she said.

Pedro served whiskies to the three men. They downed them quickly and looked toward Ollie and Rosa.

"Let's go to my office," she said.

Ollie gestured to his men to follow them as he and Rosa arose from their stools. He reached down and picked up his saddlebags, slung them over his shoulder. They all followed her toward the back. She opened the door, walked down a short hallway, opened another door with a key, and entered a lamplit office. There was a large safe behind her desk. On top of her desk was a set of scales, the brass dulled over time and splotched with dark spots.

Ollie set the saddlebags on the desk and lifted the flaps. He pulled the bags of gold dust from them and lined them up next to the scales. Rosa's eyes widened.

The music drifted into the room, muffled and distorted, but loud enough to hear. The band finished one number with loud shouts, then began another, even livelier, Mexican song, *La Cucaracha*. They could hear the patrons cheer the selection.

"I. been waitin' a long time for this," Dick

said, rubbing his palms together.

"Me, too," Red said.

"Going to cash out, Ollie?" Army asked.

"That's the idea, Army. We're splittin' five ways."

Rosa set the scales, placed a brass container on one side. She then opened the first sack and poured the dust into the bowl-like container. The scales tipped. They all looked at the number indicating the weight.

"At sixteen dollars the ounce," Rosa said, almost to herself. She marked down the weight on a piece of paper, poured the gold back into its sack and set it aside. She continued until she had weighed all the gold dust. Then she added up the figures.

Ollie peered over her shoulder. His eyes widened when he saw the number of ounces totaled up. He let out a long, low whistle.

"I'll get the money out of the safe," Rosa said, walking around behind her desk.

Just then the music stopped abruptly, and there was a loud clatter coming from the cantina. There were yells and the sounds of running boots, and a louder sound that puzzled everyone in Rosa's office.

Ollie froze. The others whirled as the noise grew louder.

Rosa gasped and threw her hands up. It sounded as if someone was tearing down the cantina, board by board, adobe brick by adobe brick.

Then there was the sound of a gunshot, and they all ducked toward the floor.

Voices rose to a high pitch, and there was no mistaking the terror behind the horrified screams.

There was another shot and the sound of stampeding footsteps and men yelling, yelling in fear as they scrambled to escape a cantina that had turned deadly.

Ollie drew his pistol. So did the others.

But none of them moved toward the door to open it.

"Do something!" Rosa screamed. "Ollie."

Ollie stood there, watching the door as if waiting for someone to burst through it. Someone he could shoot dead the minute the door it opened.

The cacophony of sounds coming from the cantina was now deafening.

Rosa shook with fear.

She pulled out a desk drawer and picked up a loaded Smith & Wesson .38 with pearl-handled grips.

She pulled back the hammer to full cock, her hand trembling.

Then, with her other hand, Rosa crossed herself, and her lips moved in a silent prayer.

22

They rode through the night like a pair of highwaymen traversing a desolate landscape in search of prey, their shirttails flapping against their cantles, the leather cinches creaking under the strain. The dappled gray looked like some ghost horse galloping past ancient gravestones that had turned to rust with dried blood, those gaunt rock outcroppings on both sides of the road, jutting up like ancient trail markers, cairns left by some long-dead traveler. And John, atop the black horse, might have been riding on air, except for the white stockings and the star blaze on the horse's long face, just below its topknot.

The Mexican blacksmith in Fountain had done a good job on Dynamite's hoof, putting a thick salve in the wound and a cushion of folded leather under the shoe before he shaped it and nailed it back on. The man's name was Guillermo Horcasitas, and he had been working late to fix a wagon wheel for a sheepherder who wanted it the next day. Dynamite favored his sore foot for a time, then began to walk without limping, so now they were riding fast, with Dynamite none the worse for wear, apparently.

They galloped and they walked, trying to push back time, gain on the men they hunted, knowing they would never catch up to them on the road, but hoping to catch them in Pueblo at Rosa's Cantina.

The air smelled of sand and creek water until the gloomy outlines of buildings appeared on the horizon and the acrid smoke of the smelters filled their nostrils, scratched their throats, and bit into their lungs with noxious fumes.

The town was half asleep, but the first person they saw, when asked, told them the way to Rosa's Cantina, and they rode there through dark streets shrouded in shadows, past lighted windows that washed them with pale yellow sprayings, and empty store windows gathered their reflections and bent them into distorted shapes that flowed like rivers in dreams and left vacancies in their wake, as if they had never passed by, nor ever existed.

Around corners and up streets they rode,

brushing past people and places they barely noticed, so intent were they on reaching their destination.

Finally, their horses breathing hard, rubbery nostrils flaring, flexing, blowing foamy mists, they saw the lights of the hotels and the cantina, and the livery sign illuminated by a lantern dangling from a standard just outside the large barn doors. They reined up in the shadows on the opposite side of the street, John and Ben breathing hard, too, holding their sides as they puffed for oxygen, and burned holes in the night with the intensity of their stares.

Three men emerged from the stables, passed under the golden light of the lantern, their legs wobbly from riding a long distance. The men headed for Rosa's Cantina, a few doors away, and John let out a breath, then drew another.

"That's them," he whispered. "That one is called Dick."

"Ollie one of 'em?" Ben asked, wheezing still, his heart pounding faster than he could think.

"No. I think that one in the middle is named Army something and the other one is Red. I can't forget him, the little bastard."

"You got good eyes, Johnny. Whew, I'm all out of breath."

"Look, they're going in to the cantina. Ollie must already be inside."

"Or maybe he's the one laggin' behind."

"We'll wait," John said. "Wind the horses some."

"Then what?"

"I've got a plan."

"Seems like you always got a plan, Johnny."

"It's always good to have one."

Ben snorted. They could hear the sounds of voices and laughter coming from the cantina. It was quiet inside the stables except for the gentle whicker of horses, the swish of hay being forked into a trough, the jingle of saddle rings, the soft slap of leather.

Five minutes passed.

"Let's tie our horses to that hitchrail in front of the hotel, then walk over to the stables," John said.

"You think Ollie's already inside the cantina?"

"I do. Makes sense he'd go in first, let his men put the horses up."

"You reading minds again, Johnny?"

"More like thinking through some things."

They rode to the front of the hotel. They could see shadows moving in the lobby, moving through gradations and layers of soft lamplight that made their features look waxen, as if they were shades risen from open caskets. They wrapped their reins around the rail.

Ben started to pull his rifle from its sheath.

"Leave it, Ben."

"Somebody might steal it."

"We won't be gone that long."

Ben snuffed puffs of air through his nostrils in exasperation. He followed John next door to the open doors of the stables. They went inside. He noticed John had his right hand dangling near the butt of his Colt.

Two men were inside. Both of them were Mexicans. One was forking hay into a stall, the other was removing the saddle from a piebald mare, the horse belonging to Red Dillard.

"You there," Johnny called. "Don't take that bridle off."

"Eh?"

"We'll need a halter on one of the others you just put up."

"But, you are not . . ."

"We know them," John said. "We're going to play a little joke on them."

"Oh, a little joke, eh?"

The man forking the hay appeared. He leaned the fork against a stall, tines buried in the straw that littered the floor.

The two men spoke in Spanish.

"Bring out the dun," John said.

"You will take just two horses?" the first man said.

"Yeah. Two is all we'll need."

The hay forker took a halter from a nail on one of the posts and entered a stall where the dun horse was chewing on lespedeza. He emerged a moment later, leading the dun. The first man handed the reins of the piebald to Ben. Ben grabbed the dun's reins.

"Now what?"

"Just follow me, Ben."

"You will be back soon, no?" the stableman asked.

"Soon," John said.

Outside, Ben stopped walking, looked at Johnny.

"Now, maybe you'll tell me what we're going to do with these two horses, Johnny. Steal them?"

John chuckled.

"We're going to run them into that cantina and start looking for those men. Especially Ollie."

"This is crazy."

"They won't expect this."

"I reckon not. You just going to start shooting once we get inside?"

"Let's see who shoots at us first."

"Crazy."

John said nothing. He got in front of Ben, strode up to the bat-wing doors. The Mexican band was in full swing. Voices rose and fell underneath the music. There was the clink of glasses, the sound of muffled laughter. John held up a hand to hold Ben in place with the two horses. Then he beckoned to him.

"I'll run the piebald in, then you whop the rump of the dun," he said. "Then, we go in."

"Behind the horses."

"Yeah, and you better stay low and have your pistol in your hand."

"Christ, Johnny."

"If that's a prayer, Ben, and not a blaspheme, it won't hurt."

John drew his pistol, moved the piebald up against the gap between the two doors. He looked back at Ben, who nodded that he was ready.

"Now," John said, stepping back, then slapping the piebald on the rump. The horse jumped ahead, parting the bat-wing doors. John stepped aside, letting Ben come on with the dun. They both slapped the rump of the dun, as the people inside yelled in surprise and confusion.

The horses panicked, tried to escape, but they were blocked by people running in all directions. A woman screamed. Men shouted at one another.

Customers, in their race to avoid the horses, turned tables over, knocked down chairs and sent spittoons spinning away like minor planets shotgunned from their orbits. A glitter girl screamed and fell over a man in a backward somersault. Two men collided head-on in the center of the room, their heads smacking together like wooden mallets.

The bartender brought out a billy club and jumped atop the bar. He drew the weapon back to smash Ben in the head. Ben whirled and fired his pistol. The bullet struck the bartender in the calf, and he crashed to the bartop, screaming in pain. The billy sailed harmlessly into the back bar, smashing bottles and glasses to glittering crystal shreds.

Two other men in the room drew pistols not five yards from John. One of them fired. His shot went wild, ploughing a furrow at John's feet. John went into a fighting crouch and fired his Colt. The man went down, his throat gushing blood onto the sawdust around the bar. The other man ran straight at John, forgetting to fire his weapon until it was too late. John brought his pistol down, cracking the man on the top of his head. Then the man's pistol fired. The bullet dug a hole two inches deep, erupting wood splinters that speared his face as he fell. He screamed in pain and dropped his pistol. John stepped on his hand, breaking his arm at the wrist.

In the office, Ollie barked orders.

"Army, get the hell out there and see what's going on. Dick, you back him up, and Red, you report back soon as you know."

The three men rushed from the room. Red glanced back at the sacks of gold. Ollie scowled at him and doubled up one of his fists. Red trailed after Army and Dick as they burst through the office door and raced down the hall.

Army stopped just short of the bar, his eyes wide in disbelief.

Dick stumbled over a man crawling on his knees and almost crashed into Army.

"That's my damned horse," he yelled.

Dick shoved Army aside and pointed to John.

"That's him, Army. Shoot him. That's the Savage kid."

Red's vision was blocked when he first entered the room. All he saw was a bunch of wild people hollering and running around like a bunch of chickens with their heads cut off. He split to the right to avoid being struck by one of the waiters heading for the rear exit. Then he jumped out of the way as the dun charged straight at him. He crashed into an overturned table, clawing for his pistol.

"Everybody out," John yelled and fought his way through the crowd. All the men at the bar ran toward the door, past Ben, who was as confused as those fleeing the stampeding horses.

The musicians dropped their instruments and fled the bandstand, all running toward the door. The piebald wheeled and charged into the crowd, scattering them like flung manikins. Some fell in a tangle of arms and legs, all yelling in fright, all clawing to get away from the slashing hooves. The dun reared up and flailed the air with his forelegs before dropping down. People streamed from the cantina, falling over each other to escape the melee.

Army drew his pistol and tried to find his target, swinging it right and left as he searched for a shooting lane. Dick brushed past him, cursing a blue streak of invective, brandishing his pistol at anyone in his path, and there were at least three innocent people between him and John Savage.

"You sonofabitch," Dick yelled and aimed his pistol at John.

John never blinked. He hammered back and squeezed the trigger of his Colt. The explosion propelled sparks of burnt powder square into Dick's face just before the bullet cracked his nose and turned his brains to mush. The back of his head flew off in a rosy spray of brains and bone that flew all the way back to where Army was standing, splattering him from head to foot.

Dick's momentum carried him almost to John's feet and he crumpled in a heap, splashing the sawdust with blood and trickle from his brain. One eye popped from its socket and glared up at John, sightless as a boiled egg.

"Get him," Red shouted as he ducked for cover behind an overturned chair near the door that led to the back office. "Shoot him, Army."

"Look out," Ben cried. "You got two of 'em aimin' right at you."

John saw Red drop behind the tipped-over table. Army was still trying to find a stationary target. But John wasn't standing still. And the two horses were looking for a way out of the chaos, running over fallen patrons and charging at walls as if trying to locate a door. Most of the people had streamed out into the street, but there were some lying on the floor, moaning, others who had been injured, crawling along the edge of the room hoping they wouldn't catch a bullet or get struck by a flying iron hoof.

Army ducked down behind the end of the bar. John saw him disappear and ran to his left, toward the center of the room. Ben kicked away a man who was trying to encircle his legs with a pair of bloody arms. The man's sleeves had been ripped off by one of the girls trying to hold on to him when the piebald kicked her halfway across the room. He lost his sleeves and then the horse kicked him with both hind feet, ripping skin and gouging holes in his shoulder muscles.

"Please help me," the man pleaded.

"Help yourself, mister," Ben growled.

John fired a shot toward Army, trying to get him to pop his head up from behind the bar. The bullet ripped across the bartop in a scream of torn wood and buried itself in the wall behind Army.

Red peered out, saw his chance, and, crouching, crabbed to the door to the back office. He slipped inside and stood up, ran down to the office.

Ollie was standing there with his pistol in

his hand. Rosa had her pistol aimed at the door.

"Almost blew you to pieces when you come through that door, Red. What the hell's goin' on out there?"

"That kid's there, and the old man, too. Dick's dead, and Army's cornered. He won't last another five minutes. Is there a back way out of here?"

"Yes," Rosa said, her voice a hiss.

"I'm lightin' a shuck," Red said. "Give me my share, Ollie. That kid'll be in here before you can say Jack Robinson."

Ollie exchanged glances with Rosa. Her eyes narrowed and she nodded slightly.

"Why, sure, Red," she said. She picked up a bag of gold dust.

Red's eyes widened. He licked his lips and holstered his pistol.

He started toward the desk.

"So long, Red," Ollie gruffed and put the barrel of his pistol square in the middle of Red's forehead. He squeezed the trigger. Red's hair caught on fire as his face collapsed under the impact of the .44 bullet. Blood spurted from his forehead and the back of his head came apart in a cloud of rosy spray. Brain matter splattered the door.

"Let's get out of here, Ollie," Rosa said quickly, stuffing the gold back in Ollie's saddlebags. "There's a door out back."

"Where we going?" he asked.

"Denver. I've got a buggy out back, the horses already hitched, and two horses tied on."

"What?"

"I planned to go away with you tonight," she said. "I just didn't know it would be like this. There's a new hotel in Denver, the Brown Palace. I made reservations for us. So we could celebrate."

They both jumped when they heard another shot.

Ollie grabbed up the saddlebags, slung them over his shoulder. Rosa took a small strongbox from the safe, closed it, and spun the cylinder, locking it.

"This way," she said.

Beyond her desk was a wall panel. Rosa pressed a recessed part of the panel and it slid open, revealing a door. She opened it and stepped aside. Ollie stepped outside. Rosa closed the panel. It slid shut smoothly. There was a Concord standing outside, four black horses hitched to it. Tied to the rear were two horses, already saddled. Ollie climbed in, then helped Rosa up. She set the strongbox on the floor, unwrapped the reins from around the brake.

"I'll drive," she said. "I know the quickest,

safest way."

"Pretty damned slick," Ollie said.

"It was my surprise for you, Ollie. I knew you'd have the goods when you came back. This team has been hitched for the last two nights."

"You're some woman, Rosa," he said.

She made a clicking sound and rattled the reins over the backs of the horses. They started out, stepping high until she put them into a canter. They wheeled down the alley, past the stables and hotels, and into the night.

Ollie leaned back, fished for a cheroot in his pocket, stuck it in his mouth.

"Under the seat, there's a lunch basket," she said. "Food and a bottle of Old Taylor."

"I can't get over you, Rosa. You think of everything."

"I hope you don't get over me, Ollie. We could go a long way together."

"What about the cantina?" he asked.

"It'll be in good hands. We'll come back when it's safe for both of us."

Ollie wondered when that would be.

He had made a mistake, not knowing that Savage kid was up in that mine. He should have killed him, along with the others. And that old man, too.

Too late now, he mused. Maybe their

paths would cross again someday and he'd get the chance to blow that kid straight to hell.

Army hunkered down as low as he could and scrunched back in the corner. He waited, holding his pistol at the ready. That last shot had torn up the bar, but hadn't even come close.

"Ben, run those damned horses out, will you?" John said as he circled the room, hunching over, using the downed tables as cover.

"Gladly," Ben replied and stepped over the man with the bloody arms. He held his pistol high and went after the piebald, first. "Everybody out," he shouted, then ran straight at the horse. It shied from him. Ben held his arms outstretched and herded the animal toward the doors. It bolted straight for them and tore both doors from their hinges as it dashed through. The dun, seeing the other horse go out that way, wheeled and galloped toward the exit, stomping two people who were lying there, their arms folded over their heads.

"Heeya!" Ben shouted as the dun cleared the doorway.

He turned back to look at John.

John was nowhere to be seen.

The room grew quiet, except for a few

moans from injured people.

Ben wondered who would break first, John or the man he had called Army.

He did not have to wait long.

John rose up from behind a tabletop near the bar. He ran toward the back door, but he was looking over in the corner behind the bar.

Army stood up then, aiming his pistol.

John fired on the run, his pistol held hip high. He thumbed the hammer back and shot again, so fast, the shots seemed to come together, with only a split second separating them.

"Damn you." Army grunted as the first bullet caught him in the belly, just above his belt buckle. He squeezed the trigger of his pistol just as John's second shot blew a hole through his rib cage and blasted his heart into blood bait for catfish. Army's eyes rolled in their sockets and remained fixed as his legs folded up and he collapsed in a heap. His gun fell into the sawdust, a tiny tendril of smoke spiraling upward from the barrel. His shot had gone high and tore a hole in the opposite adobe wall.

"That Red feller ran through that back door," Ben said. "That's likely where Ollie and that Rosa woman are."

John walked cautiously down the hallway.

The door was open to the office and Red's body lay sprawled on the floor. There was no one else in the room.

Ben came in, looked at the body.

"Right between the eyes," he said.

"That Ollie don't care who he shoots, does he?"

"They're gone, ain't they?" Ben said. "They're plumb gone."

John didn't say anything. He stood there, drew a breath and thought about how close he had come. He had gotten seven of them. But one, the one he wanted most, was still alive.

Where had he gone? Was Rosa with him? Likely, he thought.

"What are you going to do now, Johnny?" Ben asked, after several moments had passed.

John opened the gate to the Colt and started ejecting the spent shells. He stuffed fresh cartridges into the cylinders and closed the gate.

"Right now? I don't know, Ben. But I'm going to hunt Ollie down. And kill him."

"The woman, too? What about her?"

"Rosa? In a way, she was the most treacherous of all. She sat back here and let Ollie do her dirty work for her. Then she helped him escape. She's got to pay for what she did, same as Ollie."

"You'd . . ."

"Shoot a woman?"

"Yeah, I guess that's what I was going to say."

"One like her, Ben, yes. Same as shooting a snake."

John looked at the barrel of his pistol. Held it up to the light. He read the Spanish words again.

" 'Neither draw me without reason,' " he translated, " 'nor keep me without honor.' "

"Por seguro," he whispered in Spanish. He blew on the muzzle and then his lips just touched the rim of the barrel. It was like a tender kiss.

Ben stared at him and felt a sudden chill as if someone had just walked over his grave. Or someone's grave.

Maybe Ollie's. Maybe Rosa's. Maybe both.

Ben almost felt like taking off his hat and bowing his head.

It was that kind of moment.

The employees of Thorndike Press hope you have enjoyed this Large Print book. All our Thorndike and Wheeler Large Print titles are designed for easy reading, and all our books are made to last. Other Thorndike Press Large Print books are available at your library, through selected bookstores, or directly from us.

For information about titles, please call:
   (800) 223-1244

or visit our Web site at:
   www.gale.com/thorndike
   www.gale.com/wheeler

To share your comments, please write:
   Publisher
   Thorndike Press
   295 Kennedy Memorial Drive
   Waterville, ME 04901